_____ LIGHTED BRIDE

ANNE CLEELAND

For Malone's mom, who is fearless; and for all others like her.

anika braced herself inside the ornate wooden litter, her hands flat against its walls, as the carrier rocked from side to side. The renewed efforts of the six men who carried her were making the ride a bit rougher, than the usual.

She was part of a caravan that was traveling as quickly as possible, from where it had disembarked from a barge on the River Pearl, to its final destination in the hills of Canton. Nightfall came fast, here in the south of China, and the timing of this final leg of the journey had been carefully planned, so that it could be accomplished as unobtrusively as possible—just as evening fell, yet before it was too dark to navigate the steep hill up to the Hong's secluded estate.

All had not gone as planned, though; they'd encountered a bit of bad luck, in that one of the axles on a cargo wagon had broken, and they'd been forced to make a stop, so as to repair it. Kanika's outriders didn't dare leave it behind—each of these wagons was more valuable than their lives were worth.

The caravan's route, for this long journey from India to China, had been chosen to attract as little attention as possible—going overland by using the river systems, rather than sailing into the Port of Canton by ship, which could not be done anonymously —not with the British, watching the harbor so carefully. Far better to undertake the long journey by river routes, and maintain secrecy; it was hard to imagine a caravan more valuable than six wagons-full of opium, not to mention Kanika, herself, who would be considered a rare prize.

She was on her bridal journey, to be wed to a Hong, one of the powerful members of the Cohong, a group of men who'd been appointed by the Chinese Emperor to control all trade with the west. The marriage had been arranged because she was related to the Nizam of Bengal—another important figure, who wielded enormous power in his own right. Marriage to someone as well-connected as Kanika would bring her future husband almost unimaginable power and riches; unfortunately, it also meant that she was a ripe target for any man with ambitions to become a player in the immensely profitable opium trade. As it stood, the trade was closely-managed by a few, powerful people, and here was a rare chance to claim a bride who held a direct interest in the vast opium fields of Bengal.

With a finger, she pulled back the gap in the curtains, so that she had a clearer view of what was happening outside. Nothing, as yet. Hahn had ridden by on his horse a few minutes ago, and he'd glanced her way, flashing his insolent smile—which was very like him, since he tended to tempt fate, when he should be maintaining his role.

Hahn was acting as an envoy for the Nizam—or at least, everyone thought he was—and he'd been tasked with transporting Kanika from Calcutta to Canton, so as to be delivered to the Hong, her third husband. Not that she'd a second husband, of course, but—fortunately—there was no one at hand to testify to this rather surprising fact.

Due to the nature of the coming alliance, the journey was to be accomplished as secretly as possible; not only was Kanika at risk, but the mighty British would be very unhappy to discover that two of their partners in the opium trade were quietly attempting to undermine them, by funneling opium through back channels.

Out of habit, Kanika checked to make sure that her *katar* was in place, where it always rested, tied at her waist beneath her clothes. A symbol of her tribe, it was an ornamental dagger—small, so that it could be carried hidden in a hand, if necessary. It had a *shikra's* head as its hilt—one of the birds that lived in the sacred groves of Kerala, her home. It would stay hidden, of course, because the last thing a Chinese Hong would expect, would be that his exalted bride carried a symbolic weapon from a warrior tribe in southern India.

Satisfied that her dagger was secure, she waited, and contemplated the hands which were braced against the carrier—beautifully be-ringed and manicured, as befit her role. A shame, that the smaller two fingers on her right hand were scarred on the underside, but it was exactly what she deserved, for grasping hold of a hot iron railing, without realizing how hot it was. A lesson learned, for the next fire to be fled.

Pay attention, she reminded herself, as she found her mind wandering. With a quick movement, she unfastened her gold-threaded robe, and slid it off her shoulders to expose the dark, silk undergarments she wore beneath—long sleeved, and with long leggings. She then paused, to listen; any moment, now.

Suddenly, there was a loud, crack of noise like a lightning strike, and she could hear men's voices ahead of her, raised in alarm.

"A raiding party!" Hahn called out to the men. "Draw back, return fire!"

Hurriedly, the men set down the litter, as the caravan's guards began to shoot into the trees. Suddenly, an explosion erupted in the darkness up ahead—a black powder bomb, lit and hurled into their midst, so as to cause fear and confusion. Another landed on a wagon, and the canvas covering—treated with wax, so as to resist rain—promptly burst into roaring flames.

Shouting in alarm, the outriders charged toward the front of the caravan, brandishing their muskets, whilst others began beating at the fire with whatever material they could find at hand. Too late, though; opium was notoriously flammable, and the flames quickly began to devour the contents.

In the midst of the confusion, Hahn backed his frightened horse against Kanika's carrier, and drew his pistol, as though protecting her. As another bomb could be heard exploding up ahead, she quickly leapt from the carrier to the back of the horse, clinging to Hahn, and almost losing her balance, because the animal—nervous already—had startled from the sudden weight on its back.

Sitting astride, she pressed her forehead into Hahn's back, and held on tightly, as he urged his horse toward the trees that lined the steep road. Then—just as another explosion could be heard—he offered Kanika his arm, without looking at her. Grasping it, she slid from the horse's haunches, and darted into the trees.

After a quick, assessing glance, she chose a likely tree, and climbed it as rapidly as she was able, finding traction against the smooth bark with the soles of her silken shoes, which had been roughened for just this purpose.

Carefully, she then made her way ever higher, testing each branch before she transferred her weight—a breaking branch might attract attention. Fortunately, she was well-familiar with the climbing of trees, from a childhood spent in Kerala, where banyan trees were plentiful. She hadn't been nearly as important, back then—which was a good thing, all in all, since she'd been raised to think for herself, and to climb trees.

Casting a satisfied glance at the chaos which continued to unfold below her, Kanika checked her *katar*, out of habit, and then settled-in to wait.

CHAPTER 2

The next day found Kanika seated in the British Commander's office at the Port of Canton, and patiently awaiting the man's arrival, for her questioning. She'd declined an offer of tea, from one of the two soldiers who were assigned to escort her, and now she sat quietly, her hands folded and her back straight, whilst the silence stretched out.

She'd been rescued from her perch in the tree, when a contingent of British soldiers had arrived on the smoldering scene—very unhappy, of course, with what had transpired. A vast fortune, up in flames, and many uncomfortable questions raised, about what the caravan had been doing there in the first place, and trying to pass through undetected. She'd been taken to the British Compound at the port, and confined to the guest quarters, there, for the whole of the next day—

where she was shown every courtesy, but knew she a prisoner, nonetheless. And who could blame them? It seemed clear that there was a scheme afoot to undermine British interests, and gain an illicit advantage, in the workings of the valuable opium trade.

Nearly a hundred years earlier, the Chinese Emperor had allowed the British East India Company to establish a trading-base in Canton, and they'd seized the opportunity to establish a robust trade between the two countries—albeit a heavily-regulated one, since the Emperor, as well as his successors, were very wary of western influence.

Unfortunately, the East India Company had soon discovered that the most profitable import into China was opium—transported by their ships from the fields of Bengal, India—and as a result, many Chinese became addicted. The problem had become so alarming, that the current Emperor prohibited any further importation of opium, and had made strict laws against the use of the drug by his citizenry.

There was much money to be made, however, and so the wily British devised a plan to use the wealthy Chinese Cohong—a circle of prominent merchants, who oversaw western trade—to set-up a black market, so as to circumvent the intent of the Emperor's prohibition. The British would sell the opium in

Calcutta, India, and then look the other way, whilst the Cohong managed—with British contrivance—to smuggle the illegal drug into Canton.

Naturally, this situation made the Cohong very powerful, and oftentimes, its members would flex their power against the British, with the result that the opium trade was often disrupted by violence, and was balanced on the most fragile of alliances.

The British Commander at the Port of Canton was the person tasked with keeping this lucrative trade going forward, despite the hurdles imposed by the Chinese government, as well as the ruthless Cohong— who oftentimes seemed to wield more power than the Emperor, himself. By all accounts, however, the Commander was equal to the task; he was well-respected as a brilliant strategist, who managed, somehow, to keep all the various factions working together, either by brute force or by bribery, depending on whatever was needed.

But now—now, it seemed that the Commander had trouble on both ends of the trade. The Nizam of Bengal —who held authority over much of India's opium fields—had surreptitiously transported a fortune in opium overland to China, under the guise of Kanika's wedding dowry, and the Chinese Hong—her future husband—had been perfectly willing to allow the Nizam to circumvent British interests in such a way. To maintain the East India Company's iron grip on the opium trade, such a thing could not be tolerated, lest it encourage others to do the same. Therefore, the Commander's reaction had been swift and predictable; he'd ordered Kanika to be brought back to the Compound—to be held under close guard—whilst he'd gone out to investigate the scene, of this unmitigated tragedy.

In the meantime, Kanika had been allowed to wash, and change out of her smoky clothes. A guard had been sent to the Women's Quarters to fetch a plain, serviceable western gown to wear—not what she was used to, but at least the fabric was light, and comfortable. She'd smoothed her long, dark hair as best she could with her fingers, and wished she had some pins, so that she could dress it—although it hardly mattered, that she didn't have her usual embellishments; she was uncommonly beautiful, which was the whole point of her presence, here. That, and she knew how to climb a tree, of course. It was not easy to find both these attributes, in a high-caste, Indian woman.

And so now, she sat quietly in the large wooden chair that faced the Commander's desk, listening to the ticking of the clock on the wall. Into the silence, the guard told her politely, "Commander Colton should be here shortly, ma'am."

Meekly, Kanika nodded. "Thank you."

Whilst she waited, she assessed her surroundings, and decided it looked exactly as she'd expected. The Commander had a large, mahogany table that served as his desk, and there was an additional table, pushed to the side of the room and heaped with a variety of rolled-up parchments—maps, probably.

The surface of his desk was precise and ordered—he'd a desk-set, in bronze, with an inkwell and a sander, along with a quill box that was undoubtedly filled with sharpened quills, at the ready. And there—to one side, on the polished mahogany surface—was the traveling chess set; small, with the wooden figures bearing a warm patina, from having been handled so much. The pieces were set out so that it was clear that a game was in progress; she knew that he tended to play himself, when there were no worthy opponents, at hand. Covertly, she studied the board for a moment, under her lashes.

"Are you certain I can't fetch you a cup of tea, ma'am? Or perhaps a biscuit?"

With a small smile, she declined, but was pleased that he'd made the offer. She'd been informed that the British—especially the officers—were chivalrous to a fault, and after all, she was a beauty in distress. Hopefully, it would serve her well.

The door swung open, and the Commander strode

in. "Ma'am," he said politely in greeting, and cast her a quick, assessing glance.

"Sir," she replied. She did not stand, nor bow her head, because she would out-rank him, in the way the British considered such things.

He crossed the room, and seated himself behind his desk. "I trust you have come to no harm?"

"No, sir," she replied, and waited. He was much as she'd expected—tall, and broad-shouldered, nearing forty years, she guessed. He'd the rugged, no-nonsense look of a man who was used to command, and his eyes were that light blue color, that many Englishman tended to have. His hair was the color of inland sand, and he had a well-trimmed beard, that held a hint of red.

"Forgive me for keeping you waiting; there was much damage to assess."

She made no response, since she'd had a bird's-eye view of the damage—six large wagon loads, all laden with wooden chests that were packed to the brim with balls of dried opium. A vast fortune, all up in flames— save for the one chest, of course. That one would manage to make its way to the wharves of Canton, with any luck.

"I would like to ask you some questions, ma'am; will you require a translator?"

She considered. "I do not think so; my English is sufficient, I believe."

"Good. I understand that you are Nairian."

This was unexpected, but Kanika did not show by the flicker of an eyelash that she was surprised, or discomfited. "You understand correctly, sir," she replied, in her soft, precise English.

"And you were traveling to your wedding. You are betrothed to one of the Cohong."

"Yes," she agreed again, and offered, "A worthy man, I am told."

"A very wealthy man, certainly. You have not yet met him?"

"No; this is my first visit to China."

He regarded her steadily. "You may be surprised to hear that your dowry—which consisted entirely of opium, from Bengal—was illegal. It is forbidden, to transport opium into Canton."

"Oh," she said, with a show of distress, and had to reluctantly admire him for maintaining a straight face, since the British had been circumventing this prohibition on a daily basis. "Perhaps—perhaps my betrothed is not as worthy as I have been led to believe."

He did not acknowledge her remark, and asked in a direct tone, "You did not wonder, that your wedding dowry consisted of opium?""

She shook her head, slightly, in a bewildered fashion. "I am not familiar with Chinese customs—nor with the Nizam's, either. I am but a mere Nairian, you see."

She said the words with all sincerity, but she could sense he knew that she was teasing him, and wasn't very happy about it. His gaze rested on hers for a long moment, and then he tilted his head. "A Nairian, who managed to become the fourth wife of the Nizam of Bengal. A very unusual choice, in a wife."

"I am a Kshatriya," she replied, as though explaining to a child. "It is a very high caste—higher than most kings. And so, the powerful leaders in India seek to ally themselves, with women such as me." She lifted her gaze, for a moment, as though in fond remembrance. "For this reason, the Nizam treated me very kindly. He was indeed a worthy man."

"Another very wealthy man, certainly; the Nizam controls most of the opium fields in Bengal." He paused, and then added, "Unfortunately, his operations were greatly disrupted by the fire, at the Palace. The fire where he lost his life."

"I was very much grieved," she agreed, in a somber tone. "I thank you, for your condolences."

But again, he was not to be teased, and maintained a stoic expression. "You are quite the blighted bride, it seems."

She knit her brow. "I am not certain what this means."

"It means you are very unlucky."

Still frowning slightly, she considered this. "I am indeed unlucky. I must pray to my Nairian gods, for their assistance."

"Are you familiar with a Dutchman, Sir Jost Van der Haar?

Another alarming question—now she knew that he was purposefully seeking to discomfit her—but once again, she held her expression. "I am not, sir."

There was a small pause, whilst he studied her, his expression unreadable. "You have had a very trying time of it; I would ask that you remain here, as my guest—a precautionary measure, so as to ensure your safety from any further attacks. In the meantime, I will send a delegation to your betrothed, to discover if there has been a misunderstanding, about his trading agreement with the British."

"Oh," she said doubtfully. Do you think I will be safer, here? Perhaps you could take me with you, instead, so that I may be delivered to my betrothed."

"You will stay here, as a temporary measure, only," he repeated, in a tone that brooked no argument. "You command a great deal of wealth, after all, and the Hong's protection has been shown to be inadequate."

Unspoken was the obvious fact that the Hong

would be much more inclined to cooperate with the British Commander, if that self-same British Commander had custody of the man's valuable betrothed.

"Then I must thank you," she said graciously. "I am indeed tired."

"If you require anything, you have only to ask."

"Yes, sir." Gracefully, she rose to her feet. "I am pleased to make your acquaintance, Commander Colton."

He'd risen also, and now bowed, very correctly. "And I yours, ma'am."

She turned to follow her escort from the room, but not before she paused to take hold of a knight from his chess set, and move it, in a classic Bonnerjee-Indian attack gambit, before turning to walk away.

He did not move, and made no response, as she silently glided from the room.

CHAPTER 3

*A*n hour later, Kanika lay on her cot, in the guest quarters of the British Compound—a rather spartan room, as befit a military installation. She listened carefully, but could hear only silence. Her hosts had left a dim-wicked lantern on the candlestand, but she'd extinguished it, so that the room was now very dark.

Turning so that her cheek was on the edge of the straw mattress, she whispered in her native language, "Are you there?"

"I am," Hahn replied, from his hiding place, beneath her bedstead. "But I nearly fell asleep, you took so long."

"All is well?"

"All is well. Tell me what he said."

She warned, "He seems very well-informed."

"Not a surprise, Neeka. He didn't get to his position by being stupid."

"He knew I was Nairian, and he asked if I knew the Dutchman."

"Did he?" exclaimed Hahn in surprise. "Hah! He *is* well-informed. I will stay out-of-sight, then, when I go with them to the Hong's estate, tomorrow. I must be careful."

"You are never careful, Hahn," she teased, with a smile.

"Neither are you, Neeka. We will leave it for our children, to be careful."

"If we survive long enough to marry," she added, in a dry tone.

"A very good point," he agreed. "But I do not doubt it will happen—I am confident."

Again, she smiled into the darkness. "You always are, Hahn."

He was from Nair, also—although no one would guess this, because he was very good at languages, and a very clever chameleon. At present, he was passing himself off as an envoy from the Nizam, but he was equally adept at playing the role of a peasant, or even a nobleman, if such a role was called for.

He whispered, "The next marker is the attempted escape."

"Yes—I remember." There was little need for them

to communicate, from this point forward, unless she learned something that might derail the plan, or that would require some sort of improvisation.

There was a small pause, before he informed her, "Mrs. Paisley has died."

She made a sound of regret. "Ah; that is a shame. Not unexpected, of course. I hope the Reverend is bearing it well."

"I am sure that he abides," Hahn teased.

But she scolded, "You should listen to him, Hahn; he is a good man."

"I've no choice; you'll not marry me, else."

The Reverend and Mrs. Paisley were English Missionaries, originally based in Shanghai, who'd then landed in India when they'd been expelled by the Jesuits. The Reverend had then been assigned chaplain duties at Tellicherry Fort, in Kerala, which was how Kanika had first made his acquaintance.

It had been a terrible time for her people; the Nairians were storied warriors, who had not taken kindly to the British presence, in southern India. Therefore, it was only a matter of time, before the British decided to forcibly put down one of their many uprisings, and to do so with a brutal hand. A terrible purge was the result, and many of the Nairian tribesmen had been killed, in the suppression.

As a result, the British now held a firm grip in

Kerala, leaving survivors like Kanika and Hahn with a frustrated desire to wreak revenge. And that desire had been put into use by—of all things—a soft-spoken Protestant Missionary, whose benign manner hid a shrewd judge of character, and an amazing capacity to strategize.

Although he was British, himself, the Reverend had revealed to them his own burning desire to sabotage the British opium trade, along with the reasoning behind it. A righteous war, he'd explained; and wars need not always be fought with arms, and combat— especially when one's enemy was mightier, by far. Instead, other strategies were called for.

And so, gradually, a plan began to take shape—the Reverend was a very strategic planner—and, as a result of that plan, Kanika found herself here, inside the heavily-guarded British Compound at the Port of Canton, with its Commander asking his many pointed questions of her.

Hahn whispered, "I will go; I should probably drop out of sight."

"Yes," she agreed. "We should take no chances." The original plan called for Hahn to bluster and disclaim, in his pose as the Nizam's envoy, but it seemed ominous that the Commander knew more than they'd thought, and they couldn't take the chance that he'd recognize Hahn as a Nairian, too.

"I will need a diversion, then."

In response, she rose from the bed, and lifted the lantern, as she crossed over to open the door to her room.

The guard, who'd been posted outside, immediately straightened up. "Yes, ma'am?"

"I am so very sorry to disturb you, sir, but I have lost my light," she explained, and indicated the lamp.

"Let me light it, then."

He bent to do so, and Kanika noted that he could not resist taking a sidelong glance at her, standing in her western nightgown, and with her long, glossy hair unbound.

"Thank you," she whispered gratefully, and then retreated back into the room, pausing to shut the window, where the curtain was now billowing slightly.

CHAPTER 4

fter three days of patiently waiting, and with little to do, Kanika was once again summoned before the British Commander. She'd been closely-guarded, in the meantime—not that she had any desire to leave, of course—but she'd not even been allowed a maidservant to attend her, apparently for fear she'd bribe the woman to help her escape.

As a result, she'd been left to wear the plain English dress, and care for herself as best she could—no real hardship, since she'd done so much of her life; had lived in a cave, for a time, as a matter of fact. And—to the good—at least now she was well-rested, and ready for the next round with the Commander.

He stood politely at his desk, as she was escorted into his office, and she noticed immediately that he'd put the chess set away. She hid a smile, because she considered this to be a good sign, all in all.

"I trust that you have been comfortable, ma'am?" he asked, in his blunt manner.

"Yes," she replied, as she took her seat. "I thank you, for your kind hospitality."

As before, he seemed little inclined to acknowledge her gentle teasing. Instead, he announced rather abruptly, "I have spoken to your betrothed, and he is much dismayed, by the destruction of the wedding caravan." He paused. "He apologized for any misunderstanding, and tells me was not aware that your dowry would consist of opium. He assures me that he had no intent to circumvent the Emperor's edict."

"A very honest man," she remarked, with all sincerity. "I am fortunate, in my new husband."

The Commander lowered his chin, a bit. "He is a very superstitious man, I'm afraid. He is now convinced that you are unlucky."

She knit her brow, thinking about this. "He thinks I am 'blighted'?"

"Indeed. He wishes to withdraw from your marriage contract, and has asked that I convey this desire to you."

Unsaid was the obvious fact that the Commander had applied a mighty dose of pressure on the man; he could not look kindly on the possibility that the Hong's bride would continue to smuggle opium from India—it was nearly impossible to control third-party smugglers, even now, and it would be even more so, if there was wealth and organization behind such an operation.

There was a small pause, whilst Kanika digested this distressing news. "This is most unfortunate," she admitted. "What is to happen to me?"

"The Hong has given me permission to escort you back to Calcutta," the Commander explained. "We will set sail tomorrow, on *The Empress*—she makes a regular trading circuit, between Calcutta and Canton, and we are fortunate that she sails on the morrow."

"Oh," Kanika replied, and then waited for a dismayed moment, before she mustered up a smile. "Thank you for your kindness, sir."

He tilted his head. "I will confess that my intentions are not so very kind, ma'am. I will take the opportunity to speak with the new Nizam, in the event he was not aware that your—your 'dowry' consisted of fifty chests of opium. I would like to clear up any misunderstandings on that end, also."

So; as could be anticipated, the British were going to rattle their swords at the Bengal side of this disaster, too, and who could blame them? If those who controlled the opium fields in India were willing to undercut their British contracts, this could not be tolerated any more than the Hong's attempts, from the Canton side. The British held the Bengal opium growers in an iron grip, and any native insurgents who attempted to cross them would pay dearly for it. No one would know this better than Kanika, and what was left of the Nairian warriors.

As she considered this information, she lowered her gaze for a moment, as though she could not quite conceal her dismay.

Watching her, he offered, "I understand that the new Nizam is your nephew-by-marriage; a nephew to your late husband." He paused, and then added with some significance, "Is there any reason to believe your safety would be put at risk, by returning you to him?"

He was referring to the practice of *suttee*, where a deceased husband's widow would be sacrificed upon her husband's funeral pyre. It was an Indian tradition long-rooted in religious observances, and the British had made it clear they did not approve of the practice—especially when the widow controlled a great deal of wealth, and was given no choice, but to die.

"I do not know the new Nizam very well, sir," she admitted. "I cannot say what is in his mind."

That the new Nizam would find his uncle's blighted bride a hindrance—not to mention he'd be the richer, if she were dead—went without saying, and so the Commander offered, "I can return you to Kerala, if you'd prefer. Do you still have family, there?"

There was a small pause. "I do, sir. Either place, I will be welcome—please do not concern yourself."

He nodded decisively. "Kerala, then; as long as you are still on good terms, with your first husband's family?"

It was necessary to hide her surprise yet again, and Kanika did so only with a mighty effort. Oh—this Englishman was very well-informed, indeed, but if he'd hoped to discomfit her, by making the reference to her first husband, he'd misjudged his adversary, and so she replied, in all politeness, "Yes. I will manage very well, thank you."

He studied her for a moment. "Are you familiar with a Frenchman named Rochon?"

She knit her brow in puzzlement, at the unexpected turn the conversation had taken. "I am not, sir."

There was a small pause, as the candlelight flickered across his impassive face, because he wanted to make her aware that he did not necessarily believe this. The silence stretched out for a moment, and then he said, "Since you believe you have nothing to fear, then I will return you to your people with confidence. I am certain that another husband will be lined up for you in no time, and your future will be assured."

She nodded. "It is very much to be hoped, sir."

He paused, as though he wished to say something further, and then seemed to decide the better of it, and rose to his feet. "Until tomorrow, ma'am."

"Until tomorrow," she agreed, and rose to her feet, also. "Thank you, sir."

CHAPTER 5

*L*ater that night, Kanika waited by the window in her quarters, watching for Hahn's signal, and then, when she saw it, she vaulted nimbly over the window ledge, onto the ground outside. The British compound was the same as any official government compound in Canton, with the building constructed in a u-shape around an interior courtyard, and it was into this garden area that she landed, crouching down, and lifting her shawl so that it partially concealed her face.

She checked her *katar*, to ensure that it was secure against her waist, and then crept along the perimeter of the courtyard toward its entry, at the open end. When she was directly outside the window for the Commander's bedchamber, she scrutinized the ground, looking for the clay pot that should be lying somewhere in this area. There it was—good. She brought her heel down on it, and then exclaimed in startled dismay.

Almost immediately, the sentry who'd been posted at the Compound's vestibule came through the courtyard's entry, his musket at the ready. "Halt—go no further," he ordered, as he confronted her.

"Oh—oh, please, do not shoot," Kanika pleaded, and swayed slightly on her feet.

The sentry put up his weapon, and came forward to grasp her arm, so as to steady her. "What are you doing here, ma'am? The Commander won't like this at all. Here—sit down," the man said firmly, and led her over to a wrought-iron bench. "Sit here, and don't move—I'll fetch the Commander."

"No need," said the Commander, as he strode through the garden's entry in his shirtsleeves. "What's happened?"

Reluctantly, the guard admitted, "I think she was trying to escape, sir."

After casting a quick, assessing glance at Kanika, the Commander nodded briskly. "Thank you, Sergeant; I will take care of it."

The sentry departed, and there was a small silence, as Kanika could feel her companion's gaze resting upon her. She did not look at him, but instead focused on the far wall, her demeanor one of angry frustration.

The silence stretched out. "Ma'am," he finally said.

Stubbornly, Kanika lifted her chin, and allowed her exasperation to show. "I will not speak—I am tired of being polite to you."

"I can see that. Where did you plan to go?"

She pressed her lips together mulishly, and did not respond.

He repeated, "Where do you go?"

Angrily, she retorted, "I want to go home."

In a reasonable tone, he replied, "I am arranging for you to go home."

She took a long breath, as though she was trying to calm herself. "I am a pawn, in this game for power, and I am very, very tired of it."

Thoughtfully, he lifted a foot to the bench, and then bent down, resting a forearm on his knee. "I see."

With a visible effort, she lifted her face to his, and softened her voice. "Could you *please* look the other way, and allow me to go? I would offer a bribe, but I do not think you would accept it. Instead, I will ask for your mercy."

"I like the angry, damn-your-eyes version better."

Annoyed, she jerked her head away, and contemplated the far wall, again.

But his next words were unexpected. "What is it, that you have tied in the corner of your shawl?"

Still annoyed, she drew the shawl closer around her. "Nothing."

With a deliberate movement, he reached over to grasp the corner of the garment, and then extracted the fig, which had been tied within.

Holding it, he looked at her with a trace of surprise. "You truly thought to make your way, alone? I'll give you credit for courage, but you wouldn't last an hour, outside this Compound."

"I am a Kshatriya of Nair," she replied steadily. "Woe to any man, who tries to stop me."

He nodded in appreciation. "A very optimistic attitude, and I commend you for it. What was your plan?" He lifted the fig, so as to take a bite.

Stubbornly, she turned a shoulder to him. "I am not going to tell you."

"Well, I can't let you escape, as much as I sympathize. Are you worried about what your first husband's family will do, if you are returned to Kerala? Or is it Rochon, who you fear?"

"I am not going to tell you *anything*," she repeated with emphasis.

Having finished the first fig, he casually reached to lift another corner of her shawl, and extract a second one.

In exasperation, she protested, "You are eating all my food—it was not easy to hide it."

His hand paused, and then he offered the fig to her.

Despite herself, she couldn't resist a small smile, as she accepted it. "I thank you," she said, with as much dignity as she could muster.

He was silent for a moment, as he watched her bite into the fruit, and then he said, in a serious tone, "You think to escape, still—I can see the calculation in your eyes. I understand how it feels—to make a plan, and gather your courage to execute it, and then to be frustrated, at the last minute. But I have more experience in such things, and I have learned that— sometimes—you must abandon your plan, if it is no longer feasible. I'm afraid this is one of those times."

She frowned slightly, and fingered the fig in her lap, her head bent. "I do not wish to be a pawn, anymore— useful only for the husbands that I can attract. I am clever, and I can avoid being caught. I promise, that I will do nothing foolish, if you would *please* let me go. I would never tell anyone that you did so."

"You are clever, and brave," he agreed. "Small wonder, that you have managed to attract the string of husbands that you have."

She eyed him, sidelong. "You seem to know much about me." He did, and it was a little alarming, all in all.

"It was my business, these past few days, to discover as much as I could," he readily admitted.

"Although I am not at all clear on how a Nairian woman—no matter how high her caste—would be willing to become the fourth wife of the Nizam of Bengal."

She took a breath, as though weighing whether to tell him, and then admitted, "My people—those who were left—sought protection from the British. An alliance was necessary—an alliance with someone who would be as powerful as the British."

"No one is as powerful as the British," he pointed out, in a practical manner.

"Perhaps, perhaps not. But an alliance was necessary, in order to survive."

"And so, you were the sacrifice."

She glanced up at him, and slowly shook her head. "It wasn't a sacrifice—not at all; I was more than willing, to help my people. And the Nizam was a kind man. He liked to play chess, with me."

For the first time, she could discern a glint of humor, in his eyes. "Did you let him win?"

She hesitated. "Most times," she admitted.

He brushed his hands, and straightened up. "Well, if it's any consolation, I'd like to play with you, too, and I would ask that you do not let me win, if I deserve to lose. I imagine that we will have plenty of opportunity, aboard *The Empress*."

Pressing her lips together in acute disappointment,

she looked away. "You are not going to let me go, then."

"No. I am sorry. I will keep you safe, though—my promise on it."

"A bold promise," she noted, rather dryly.

Hearing the irony in her tone, he ducked his head in reluctant concession. "I will do the best I can. If you truly think you are going to come to harm, you can always refuse to go back to India."

"I can't stay here," she replied, a bit crossly. "I hate it, here."

He held out a hand, to help her rise to her feet. "I will tell you a secret, Kshatriya of Nair; so do I."

CHAPTER 6

Because Kanika's attempted escape had diverted all attention to the courtyard, Hahn had once again managed to secret himself beneath her bedstead, so as to conduct another whispered conversation, once the compound had settled into sleep.

"It went well, from the looks of it. You are a wonder, Neeka." He'd been on the roof, no doubt, and watching them; thin and wiry, Hahn could scramble over the tiles like a shadow.

"Yes; I think it went well," she agreed. She decided not to mention that speaking to the Commander had reminded her of the time when she'd grasped the hot railing, without realizing it was going to burn her.

"Are any adjustments needed?"

"No—I don't think so," she whispered. "Tell me, Hahn, who is 'Rochon'"?

"I don't know. Why?"

She frowned into the darkness. "He keeps mentioning the name, and then watches for my reaction."

But her companion did not seem discomfited by this news. "All the better, if he believes you have alliances, and thinks he can predict what you will do."

"I suppose that is true. I think—I think he believes I was trying to escape, not necessarily because of what will happen to me, if I am returned to India, but because I greatly fear this Rochon person."

"Oh?" Hahn considered this. "I don't think it matters, as long as the Commander believes you are in danger."

"Yes." After a moment's reluctance, she added, "He promised he would keep me safe."

Hahn made a sound of satisfaction, and—hearing it —she chided herself for hesitating to tell him this. She needed to keep Hahn informed, and just because she'd been rather touched by the promise, it was no reason to lose sight of their aim.

"It is just as the Reverend said—the English are very predictable. Now the Commander will feel he has no choice but to come to your aid; it is a weakness, to be exploited."

She warned, "Yes, but have a care, Hahn; this Englishman is very shrewd."

"Not shrewder than me," Hahn declared, teasing.

She smiled, slightly. "He wishes to play chess, with me."

Very pleased yet again, her companion said, "Even better; we know he used to play with his wife."

The Reverend had gleaned this information from the network of Missionaries, who were scattered throughout China and the subcontinent; oftentimes their very lives depended upon staying well-informed, and so the various Christian clergy exchanged any information that might be important, with respect to this rather volatile area of the word. Through his contacts, the Reverend had learned some very useful information, along with the fact that the Commander's late wife had been a graceful, demure woman, with long, black hair.

Thinking on this, Kanika confessed, "I feel—I feel a bit sorry for him, I suppose. He doesn't seem an evil man—not like so many of the others."

To his credit, Hahn considered this without chiding her—Hahn was of all things reasonable, which was why the Reverend had recruited him; in general, Nairian tribesmen tended not to be reasonable, which was why there weren't very many who were left alive.

"No matter what he says or does, Neeka, he is their

key man, in the opium trade—he runs everything, like clockwork. There is nothing honorable about what he is doing."

"Yes; I know." It was on the tip of her tongue, to tell Hahn that the Commander said that he hated being here, but she refrained. He'd said it was a secret, and—strangely enough—it would feel like a betrayal. Not that she had any allegiance to him, of course; but still, she'd keep his confidence.

Hahn added, "The English are very efficient—and that is the problem."

"Yes, I know, Hahn. Please don't think me foolish; I only mentioned it, because it was unexpected—that he was so courteous."

"You do not sound convinced—you will make me jealous," he teased.

"No—no, of course not," she replied with a smile, and wished that this was true. There was no denying that there had been something between them—the Commander, and herself—and that it had resonated like a plucked bow-string, when he'd handed her the fig.

"I'll go—I need my sleep. The next marker is the wharf riot."

"Yes—I remember. Do you need a diversion?"

"No—we can't do it twice, or the guard will be suspicious. I will make my own way, this time."

He sidled out from under the bed, and walked on cat's feet over to the window, where he watched the guard at the vestibule for a moment—timing his actions—and then stood upon the sill, so as grasp the eave above him, quickly pull himself up, and disappear out of sight.

The next day, Kanika was transported her to the docks that lined the mouth of the Pearl River. Relieved to finally be away from the confines of the British Compound, she stepped from her litter, and looked around with interest, at the sights that surrounded her.

The British trading presence in China had been narrowly circumscribed to this small wharf in the Bay of Canton and—as a result—it was bristling with ships, many of them anchored temporarily in the Bay, and a few taking turns at the makeshift dock, where they loaded up on goods that had been carried over from the warehouses by an army of Chinese workers. Heavy chests were then unloaded or loaded into cargo holds by wooden pulley structures, all accomplished with amazing speed, so that the next ship could quickly take its place. It was an impressive operation by the British, considering the constraints that had been placed upon them, and Kanika knew a moments unease, that the enemy was capable of producing such an undertaking, out of the small port access that they'd been grudgingly granted.

The Reverend had told them that England was not a large country—not compared to India—but that the people were very industrious, and clever. You could see evidence of this—here, and back in Kerala, also; between brute force and enticements, the English had managed to obtain control over a population many times its size, and located all the way over, on the other side of the world. It was alarming, and rather ominous, and the very reason that the Reverend had sought to develop his plan.

Kanika had been assigned two British soldiers as escort—the Commander was taking no chances—and she stood between them, as they awaited instructions. There were several East India Company ships positioned along the dock—the largest one being *The Empress*—and Kanika almost immediately spotted the Commander, standing next to the ship's gangway, and speaking to a man she presumed to be the ship's Captain.

Upon sighting Kanika, the Commander approached her. "Good morning, ma'am. We will set sail in an hour's time, but I will have you boarded now, if you don't mind. If you would stay below, and out of sight, it would be for the best."

"Yes, sir," she said meekly.

He gave her a look, to let her know that he was well-aware that her show of mild obedience was just that, but then he took her elbow, to lead her aside for a moment, and out of earshot.

Carefully, Kanika hid her discomfiture at his actions; where she was from, men did not touch women who were not related to them—and certainly did not draw them away, so as to speak privately. And—Kanika decided—there was good reason for this, since the gesture seemed rather intimate, and inspired some rather unsettling feelings, within her breast.

Whilst his sharp gaze continued to assess the loading activity, the Commander bent his head to hers, and said in a quiet tone, "I have been thinking about it, and if you have any concerns about your safety—any concerns at all—then I can put you aboard a ship bound for London, out of Calcutta. You needn't set foot in India, if you'd rather not."

"I would go to London?" Kanika asked, in some surprise.

"Yes. There is a fairly large Indian population, in London, and you should encounter no difficulties, if you wished to settle there. It may be the best solution, for a woman in your situation."

Since this unlooked-for development was a potential problem, in carrying-out the Reverend's plan, Kanika tried to decide how best to counter this suggestion. Before she could fashion a response, however, their conversation was interrupted by a series of shouts from the dock before them, as a wooden chest that was being loaded onto the ship broke from one the pullies, that held it aloft. After dangling atilt for a moment or two, the remaining pulley gave way, and the cargo chest then crashed down onto the dock.

The impact caused the hinges to break, and the contents were exposed as they spilled onto the dock— hundreds of opium balls, packed tightly together.

With a startled curse, the Commander called "Watch her," to Kanika's escorts, and then strode toward the chaos, calling for the soldiers who were posted along the docks to keep order. It was too late, however; a handful of the opium balls would be worth many a month's wages, and the Chinese workers scrambled and fought to scoop up the treasure.

The shouts and scuffles began to escalate, and the British soldiers waded into the melee, firing their weapons overhead. Turning to the Captain, the Commander shouted, "Cast off; no one boards the ship."

He then turned to Kanika's guards. "Quickly; take her back to the Compound, and tell the garrison we'll need another platoon."

At her guards' urging, Kanika was then bundled back into the litter, which was quickly hoisted aloft, by its Chinese carriers. She was then hurried back to the British Compound, her guards running alongside with their weapons at the ready, in the event there was more trouble, to be had.

CHAPTER 8

It was two days later, and it could be presumed that the uprising on the docks had been quelled. Kanika hadn't heard from Hahn, because he'd have his hands full, and they dared not take the chance that he'd be caught communicating with her, now that security had been heightened around the British Compound.

Since she'd been thoroughly sequestered—and heavily guarded—Kanika didn't know what had been going forward, only that she'd the general sense that tensions continued high, since there were more soldiers than there were before, posted at the Compound. The wharf riot had ominous overtones, certainly; under the terms of the prohibition, the British were not allowed to export opium from the Canton docks, and the Emperor's representatives—stationed there, to keep an eye on such things—would be asking some very uncomfortable questions, of the British Commander.

In the meantime, Kanika was left with no choice but to abide in patience, and await events. Fortunately, it seemed that her boredom was soon to come to an end, because when the usual guard delivered her evening meal, he advised, "The Commander has requested that you join him to play chess this evening, ma'am. He sends his apologies for your isolation these past two days, but felt it was necessary, for your safety."

She smiled in gratitude. "Thank you; I would very much enjoy leaving this room, even if I were to be put to cleaning the floor."

The young guard returned her smile. "I doubt that will be necessary," he joked.

He is nice enough, she decided, as he set the tray down on her bedside table, *but he's not going to come to my aid, if I asked him, which is probably why he has been given this task. I cannot fault him for it; loyalty is something to be admired, especially in these current times.*

After she finished her meal, she was escorted into the Commander's office, where he stood beside his desk, and bowed his head in greeting. The chess set had reappeared, and had been set up crosswise on the corner of the desk, so that she could reach it easily, from her chair.

"Good evening," he said. "I trust that you are well,

ma'am?" He presented his closed hands, so that she could choose which pawn color was to be hers.

"Sir," she greeted him, and chose the hand that was revealed to hold the white pawn. "I hope that your people did not suffer too greatly, from the troubles on the wharf."

"That remains to be seen," he replied in an even tone, as he saw her seated, and then walked around to take his own seat. "Unfortunately, I have been asked a great many questions about why opium was being loaded onto one of the Company's ships, and why it was only happenstance, that the Emperor's representatives became aware of this."

"It is indeed very concerning," she acknowledged with all sympathy, and moved a pawn.

He moved a pawn in response. "I had to confess to them that I could not find a bill-of-lading, for the broken chest, and so I sent an inquiry to your former betrothed, in the event the chest was one that had originated from your dowry—it seemed very similar."

She lifted her head to meet his gaze, her own brow knit. "I don't understand; I thought my dowry had been destroyed."

"Apparently, not all of it."

She lowered her gaze to the board, again. "It makes little sense; surely, the Hong would not send opium back to India?" She moved another piece.

He studied the board. "The Hong has denied any knowledge of it, and seemed offended that the question would even be asked. When pressed, however, he speculated that the new Nizam in Bengal may have orchestrated both the fire that destroyed your dowry, as well as this broken chest, in an attempt to undermine the Hong's relationship with the Company."

She stared at him in surprise. "Then, the Nizam arranged for my betrothal, only as a means to ruin my husband-to-be?"

"Your husband-to-be appears to believe that this may be the case."

"Why, that is terrible," she declared, in all concern.

As he studied the board, her companion replied, "It remains to be seen; it may be that the Hong is attempting to cast blame elsewhere. There is no denying that he was perfectly willing to marry you, which seems rather suspicious, in its own right."

She shook her head, slightly, and deftly picked up one of his pawns with slim fingers. "It is of all things unfortunate, that they should so distrust one another; my betrothal was intended to build an alliance, not to create ill feelings."

"Do you know anything, of these matters?" he asked, in a deceptively polite tone.

Regretfully, she shook her head. "I do not. But I am

very much shocked, that I would be used, in such a way. I am a Kshatriya of Nair, and it is very disrespectful."

"I have every confidence that I will discover who is using whom," he replied, a trace of irony underlying his words. "And then, I will put an end to it. I will have your knight, I think."

She relinquished the piece with good grace. "It is very much to be hoped," she offered. "Otherwise, you may be thought to be as unlucky as I."

As she moved her rook's pawn, she could sense that he was amused by her sincere-but-insincere manner, despite himself. He offered, "I don't believe in luck—good or bad. And I don't believe in coincidences, either. It seems very strange, that a trail of disaster seems to follow you."

"I am indeed a blighted bride," she observed a bit sadly, and countered his move.

His assessing gaze lifted to study her for a moment, before he bowed his head, to continue with his study of the board. "I would advise that you not make mention of this trail of disaster to your next husband."

"This is very good advice," she agreed, and moved her rook.

He paused, and then leaned against the arm of his chair, so as to regard her seriously, for a moment. "Tell me the truth, if you please; do you think you are at risk for *suttee*?"

This was blunt speaking, and she rather appreciated it—although the verbal fencing was also very entertaining. "I do not know, sir."

"But you fear going home."

With a slight frown, she chose her words carefully. "I have been shown to be unlucky, as you have said, yourself. My people tend to be superstitious, and— even though I am a Kshatriya—it is a concern. There is every possibility that I will be shunned." She paused, and then added in a subdued manner, "And, I am merely a woman, so I must fear everything."

In a dry tone, he advised, "That's not working; you'll never convince me you fear anything."

She smiled, slightly, and moved her queen. "You like 'damn-your-eyes' better."

"I do, only because I think it's more in keeping."

"You are correct," she admitted. "But I must be careful; I cannot create ill feelings, in my present circumstances."

There was a small silence, as he made his next move, and then, again, he spoke bluntly. "If the new Nizam was complicit, in this smuggling scheme, then he has a very fine reason to be rid of you, so that you do not tell the tale of how it all came about."

"Then, we must hope that such is not the case," she replied.

He pressed, "But you fear it is so; you were going to flee, rather than take the chance of being hauled before him."

Without answering directly, she said, "It is as I told you; I do not wish to be a pawn, anymore." She scooped up one of his pawns, for emphasis.

He took a long breath, as he studied the board for a moment. "I am afraid that I have no choice, but to bring you before him, in light of the Hong's accusations. However, I will seek assurances for your safety; the Company carries a great deal of weight, with the new Nizam, and—presumably—he will do as I ask."

"Thank you, sir," she said absently, as she studied the board.

There was a small silence. "My name is James," he offered.

She met his eyes in surprise. "I cannot address you by your given name," she explained. "Such a thing is forbidden."

As though she hadn't spoken, he asked, "What is your given name?"

"I should not tell you," she protested, unable to resist a smile. "You are very bold."

"Tell me," he insisted. "I won't let anyone know you've done something so shocking."

Hesitating, she relented. "Kanika."

He leaned back in his chair; his brows drawn together, and the game forgotten, for the moment. "Then it *is* you," he said. "I will confess that I was having my doubts."

Suddenly wary, she returned his regard. "I do not understand."

"Sir Jost warned me that you were ruthless, and that I should be very much on my guard."

"Oh." She contemplated this, and admitted fairly, "I can see why he would think this."

"He did show me a scar."

"I caught him, unaware," she admitted. "He would not let it happen again, I think."

He seemed amused, and allowed a smile to play around his lips. "Why all the playacting, then? What is your aim, in all this?"

She met his gaze, in all surprise. "Did not I say? My people had to ally with the Nizam, so that the British would not be tempted to destroy what was left of us."

He continued to regard her thoughtfully, and offered, "It must have come as quite a blow to your plans—that the Nizam's Palace burned down, and he died in the fire."

"Very unlucky," she agreed. "And so, my marriage

to the Hong was quickly arranged, so as to find another source of protection for my people."

He tilted his head. "Not to mention that the Hong would be happy to seize the chance of a back-channel opium trade, with the new Nizam."

Gently, she chided, "I prefer to think that he was pleased to align his ancestral house with a Kshatriya of Nair—it would bring much prestige, to him."

"A Kshatriya of Nair, who has a direct connection to the opium fields of Bengal, and who also happens to be young and beautiful," her companion countered, with a tinge of irony. "You can hardly blame the Hong; it would be a difficult proposal to turn down."

"I thank you, sir," she said politely, ignoring his ironic tone.

He bent forward, so as to study the board again, and they resumed the game in silence. He was a very good player—not as bold as she, but methodical—and she was quite enjoying the opportunity; it had been some time, since she'd last played with the Reverend. Although, if the Reverend were here, he would easily beat the both of them.

"So; you lied, when you told me you didn't know Sir Jost."

"Yes," she agreed, without a twinge of guilt.

He studied the board without looking at her. "More

correctly, it was your husband, who was acquainted with him, I believe. Your first husband."

Debating, Kanika decided that she may as well tell the tale—it seemed clear that the Commander knew much of it, already, and she should probably test it, to see how much—exactly—he did know, in the event she needed to warn Hahn. With this in mind, she sat back, and folded her hands on her lap.

CHAPTER 9

The steady candlelight reflected off her companion's face, as he waited to hear what she had to say—his expression very serious. She found his rapt attention very pleasing; in her experience, men did not pay much attention to women, save for the Reverend—and Hahn, of course. But she mustn't be flattered, and instead she must remember that he was a very clever man, and that she must step carefully—no matter how enjoyable it was, to speak with him thus.

She began, "I married Abhay when I was very young, as is the tradition, with our people. He was the son of a Nairian chief—a very respected lineage—and so the alliance was to the benefit of both families." She paused for a moment, and explained, "Abhay was—he was quick-tempered, and brash. And—like so many young men—he was very unhappy, with the British rule in Kerala. He plotted to attack a British garrison, but was caught, and sentenced to be indentured, aboard a British ship. But then, the ship was captured by the Dutchman, during the time when he was a pirate. Abhay was very happy to join-in with him, and they attacked the British, together. They became very good friends."

The Commander continued to listen without comment, and so she continued, "Abhay and the Dutchman were part of a *niyama*, along with two other men." She knit her brow, trying to find the words to explain. "It is a promise—very sacred—that if any of them died, the others would look after the families."

"I see," he prompted. "And then?"

"The Dutchman changed his mind, about being a pirate—I am not certain why." Frowning, she shook her head, slightly. "He decided that he would help the British with their trading, instead of stealing from them —it was very, very surprising. Abhay could not agree, of course, and so they parted ways, with Abhay returning to Kerala." She paused. "Abhay was then killed, during the—the uprising." Diplomatically, she did not mention that he'd been killed by British forces, who'd been required to fight fiercely, in order to suppress the Nairian uprising. The Commander would know this, without her saying.

"I am sorry," he said, with all sincerity.

She nodded in acknowledgment, and then continued. "After Abhay died, the Dutchman came to find me, on account of the *niyama*. Even though he and Abhay were no longer friends, he would honor his oath."

"It didn't work out very well for Sir Jost, I gather."

She nodded, unrepentant. "I was not going to have anything to do with him—not only did the Dutchman take Abhay away from his people, he then joined-in with the British, and betrayed him. He is a devil, and so, I stabbed him, with my *katar*." She paused, and then added, as explanation, "It thirsts for the blood of the wicked."

His eyes remained level, fixed upon hers. "Do you still carry this *katar*?"

She stared at him, stricken. *Neeka,* she thought, in acute dismay; *you are a fool.*

He offered, "I won't take it, if you promise you will not use it against me, or my men."

Slowly, she shook her head. "A Nairian cannot make such a promise."

He nodded. "Then we will pretend we never spoke of it."

She nodded in response, and found, for a moment, that she was unable to find her voice. To cover for this lapse, she bent her head, working to control her emotions.

"What happened with Sir Jost? Aside from the scar?"

Composed, she lifted her face again. "He left to search for my husband's sister, Aditi. She was part of the *niyama*, also."

But her companion had brought his brows together, in profound surprise. "*Aditi Landon* is your sister-in-law?"

She stared at him in puzzlement, and then shook her head, slightly. "I don't understand what it is you are saying."

"If it is the same girl, she is now married to an Englishman, and lives in London."

Astonished, she exclaimed, "Aditi? I do not think it can possibly be the same girl. Aditi was not—" here, she paused, trying to decide what to say. "She was headstrong, like Abhay. And she chose to be a concubine—she was not a woman that a man would wish to marry."

He cocked a brow. "Sir Jost is the one who brought her to London, along with her new husband."

"This is true?" Kanika exclaimed in wonder. "Then it is indeed my husband's sister—I am amazed."

"A small world," he said.

"A small world," she repeated thoughtfully, guessing at the meaning.

"We are going to play to a draw," he advised.

"Yes," she agreed, her attention recalled to the board.

"Shall we play again?"

No, no, no, Kanika thought immediately, but unfortunately, her words didn't seem to be obeying her mind. "Yes. Another game, please."

The Commander set-up the board again, and made the first move, since she'd been first, last time. *I don't think either one of us is concentrating on the game,* she thought; *and so, I imagine another draw will be the result.*

Into the silence, he said, "Before he had his change of heart, Sir Jost used to run opium, on his ship."

"The Dutch were the ones who started the opium trade," she agreed, in a severe tone. "And they should be cursed for it, many times over."

As though she hadn't spoken, her companion continued, "He ran opium for Rochon, which turned out to be very useful, for the British; Sir Jost knew a great deal about Rochon's operations, so that we could put a stop to them."

The words hung in the air, and despite Hahn's advice, Kanika decided to be honest. Meeting his eyes, she shook her head slowly. "I do not know this 'Rochon' you keep mentioning. I do not fear him."

He studied her, for a silent moment. "I don't know as I believe you. You are a very good liar."

"Yes," she agreed. "But nevertheless, I do not know this Rochon."

"Then whom do you fear? The new Nizam? Your own kinfolk?"

"My kinfolk will not welcome me back," she admitted. "I am twice-widowed, and now I have been rejected by my third husband. I will be considered shamed."

This was, in fact, a real concern—and one of the reasons the Reverend had suggested that she and Hahn marry, after the plan was completed. No other Indian man would wish to, no matter her status, or her beauty.

The Commander suggested, "It is not too late to seek Sir Jost's protection; he is married himself, now, and has a plantation in the West Indies. Or—as I said—I can see you safely settled in London."

"Neither course is acceptable," she replied, firmly. "I will be beholden to no one."

But he tilted his head slightly. "I am not going to allow you to do anything foolish, Kanika."

Her eyes flew to his in surprise. "You mistake me, for someone who cannot decide such things for herself. Although you can be forgiven, for thinking that no one dares to say 'no', to the mighty British, and their opium riches."

She could see that this stung him, but he replied in an even tone, "The mighty British are needed to defeat Napoleon. The money from the opium trade is necessary to fund the war."

In confusion, she knit her brow slightly, trying to remember what she'd heard. "There is a war, in Europe."

He nodded. "There is, indeed—although there's been a pause, for the time being. Napoleon must be stopped, or England will fall."

"A terrible tragedy," she offered. "I weep, to think of it."

He nodded slightly, in acknowledgement. "You see a side of England that is—that is not necessarily the finest. But believe me, England is a force for good, in the world, and if Napoleon is successful, many will suffer for it. He has twice the army England has, and so England has to pay for mercenaries, to help them fight the war. A great deal of money is needed, for this reason. The Indian opium is swapped for Chinese tea, and then the tea sells for a very high price, in England."

She thought about this, having never heard the explanation, before. "So; you must be ruthless, because you believe the ends justify the means."

"Yes," he said, without remorse. "I do believe it, or I wouldn't be a part of it. And remember, that no one is being coerced, here; there is a demand for a product. The people who use opium make that choice."

But this touched on a very sore subject, and leaning forward, she retorted in a heated tone, "But your ends are not healthy for my people, sir. We have suffered greatly, from your opium trade, because the people are starving—the British pay the farmers so much money for opium, that they won't plant any other crops, and now there is not enough food."

"They cannot be blamed, surely? It is a valuable crop, for them."

Her brows drawn together fiercely, she returned, "But it is an evil crop; the people become lazy, and senseless; smoking their opium, and forgetting their obligations."

He bent his head in acknowledgment, but repeated, "Everyone must make their own choices. And in the end, the money is needed for the greater good."

But she could not agree, and quoted what the Reverend had said. "There will be much bloodshed, over this cursed crop; wars fought, and many lives lost."

Steadily, he replied, "I would not be surprised. It is always the way, where there are riches to be gained— and gained rather easily, in this case."

Their eyes locked for a long moment, in the silent room, with the candlelight flickering, until she said, "I think you are a hard man, sir."

"I think many would consider you a hard woman."

She had to smile at this, and the tension was broken. "You forget that I am Nairian—it is a compliment."

He'd apparently decided that he wasn't behaving well, and offered in a more conciliatory tone, "I beg your pardon, if I was too harsh. I will admit it is a difficult subject to defend."

"Then we will call a draw," she suggested. "I am sorry, too."

With a glint in his eye, he observed, "It makes me wary, when you make a show of meekness. Promise that you will not try to escape again, and in turn, I will promise to see to your safety."

"I will think about it," she demurred, and rose gracefully to her feet, which obligated him to rise, also. "Good night, sir."

"Good night," he replied, and walked across the room to call for her escort.

Silently, Kanika walked back to her room beside the guard, who interrupted her thoughts to disclose, "The bookseller delivered the book you'd asked for, ma'am. I left it in your room—the Commander won't allow tradesmen to come within the Compound."

"Thank you," she said. "It is greatly appreciated."

Bidding him good night, she then walked over to her bedside table, and found the small volume of Chinese fables. She opened the book, and inscribed on the flyleaf were the words in her own language, *The next marker is the fire.*

Ah yes—another fire, she thought to herself, with a mental sigh. I hope it turns out better, this time; my fingers did not much enjoy the last one.

CHAPTER 10

The Compound had settled into silence, and Kanika lay on her cot, contemplating the sliver of moonlight that streamed into the room, through a small part in the curtains. She was having trouble falling asleep—there were many things to consider, and she couldn't help dwelling on the conversation she'd had with the Commander, and trying to remember what he'd said to her, and in as much detail as she could remember.

It was very surprising, that he'd spoken of the need to fund a war, with the opium money—she'd never heard this explanation before, and it made him seem a little less ruthless. He believed his country was at risk, in the same way that she believed her country was at risk, and so they were both taking action, and doing what they thought was necessary.

What he is doing is much worse, though, she reminded herself sternly. *He runs an evil trade, that is destroying many, many lives. Surely there are other ways to make money, so as to pay the soldiers.*

And it was already something of a sore subject, for her, because she'd heard a similar explanation from Abhay—on those rare occasions, when he'd visited his young wife. He'd brought home riches, from his piracy with the Dutchman, but then he'd used most of those riches to constantly attack the British, at great cost to his people, as well as the loss of many lives.

Was it worth it? Kanika could not think so, and indeed, it was one of the reasons she'd been so drawn to the Reverend, after her husband—and so many others—had been massacred, and she'd been forced to hide in a cave from the Dutchman.

The kindly Missionary and his wife had taken her in, and their gentle manner had acted as a balm to her wounded soul. Her people had suffered terrible losses, and their words—words of peace, and hope—struck a chord within her; certainly, the old ways did not seem to be working.

The Reverend had played chess with her for hours —he was a very skilled player, even more skilled than her father had been—and he gradually began to speak of the plan, that he'd hatched. He felt that the opium trade was the work of the devil, and since Kanika already equated the devil with the English, she was more than willing to listen. It was a simple plan—bold in its very simplicity—and required only an attractive, high-caste woman, to set it in motion. The problem being, of course, that an attractive, high-caste woman would not even be allowed to speak to the Reverend, let alone agree to participate in his plan.

And so, the Reverend had said, it was a sign from God, that Kanika had practically fallen into their laps, and she could only agree with this assessment, as she willingly converted to his religion.

She would have allies, but only a few—the smaller the circle, the better. Hahn was the perfect choice, in that she'd known him since childhood; he could be trusted, and he was not as headstrong as Abhay had been—instead, he was many times more clever. Since Kanika would necessarily be shunned from society, after the plan came to completion, the Reverend had suggested that they agree to be married. They couldn't marry immediately, the Reverend explained, because in her role, Kanika may be called upon to commit adultery, which would be a grave sin, if she were married to Hahn.

And the plan had worked flawlessly, so far—the Reverend was an excellent chess player, after all. Save for the unexpected development that Kanika felt herself drawn to the British Commander, of course. It was the last thing she'd expected, and it rather complicated things.

We are very much alike, she acknowledged. *I know it, and he knows it, too. It is why we can't help but treat each other as equals, despite our genders, and our castes—and everything else.*

And he was drawn to her, too—she could feel him fighting it, beneath his restrained manner. In fact, she had the sense—when he'd mentioned London, as a potential destination for her—that it was because he wanted to arrange to see her, again, away from the constrictions that were placed upon her, here.

Which made little sense; the reason he'd obtained his high position—even though he was not an aristocrat, and such positions were usually reserved for such—was because he was very good at what he did. As Hahn had said, he was their key man, in the opium-trading operation; efficient, and able to piece together the vying factions into one efficient mechanism, despite the hurdles thrown his way by the disapproving Chinese Emperor. Indeed, the Reverend himself had noted it was a shame, that the usual aristocratic second-son had not been appointed to the Commander's position. Aristocratic second-sons tended not to need any outside intervention, to set things into disarray.

But—despite the fact that the Commander was

well-respected, and performing admirably in his appointed task—unless Kanika's instinct was wrong, the Commander was longing to be away from it, and return to England. That first night, in the garden, he'd told her that he hated it, here—which was a surprising confession to make, and only proved that she'd penetrated his defenses, and rather quickly, at that.

She knew he'd been married for nearly ten years, but that his wife had died, childless. The Reverend—who'd discovered a great deal, through his Missionary network—could find no indication that the Commander had taken a concubine, in Canton, which was somewhat surprising, since it would be a matter of course, for most men—even Abhay had taken a concubine, when he'd been away from home for so long, sailing with the Dutchman.

The Reverend surmised that the man grieved for his late wife, and so Kanika had been schooled to portray a meek manner—that the Reverend assured her was very English—so as to awaken his chivalric instincts.

I am not sure it is working quite the way the Reverend intended, she admitted to herself, unable to suppress a smile. *The Commander sees through the façade, and lets me know that he sees through it. It amuses the both of us, actually.*

So; she was attracted to the Commander, but in the

end, she mustn't be deterred from the goal, and the goal was fast becoming a reality—amazing, that a simple Missionary had mapped out a plan—based on little more than his knowledge of how people tended to behave—and he'd been proved right, in almost every aspect.

If she were honest with herself, though, she'd admit that when the Commander had mused aloud about bringing her to London—twice—her heart had leapt, a little. *Foolish girl,* she chastised herself. *You are betrothed to Hahn, and besides, the Commander is an Englishman, and you'd hate living amongst the English—enough. In this instance, at least, the ends do indeed justify the means.*

She then turned over, and tried to put her mind to sleep. Another marker, tomorrow—a big one—and she'd need to have her wits about her.

CHAPTER 11

For the second time, Kanika stood on the dock before *The Empress*, awaiting her departure on the tide, and watching as the cargo was uploaded onto the ship's deck, for delivery into the cargo hold. She noted that security had been heightened, along the wharf—additional British soldiers had been posted to maintain order, and she also saw that the Chinese had added their own representatives, so as to keep a sharp eye on the cargo. Good; tensions were palpably high, and the workers seemed more subdued, than the last time they'd tried to launch.

This time, however, she was escorted on board without incident, and shown to her cabin, which was very cramped, with barely enough room to hold a bunk and a small cupboard, to secure her bag. Not that she'd much baggage, of course, but no matter; she wouldn't be staying here long, after all.

After waiting for perhaps ten minutes, she opened her cabin door, and signaled to the sailor who'd been posted to guard her. "If you please, sir," she said in her soft voice, her eyes wide, "I must speak to the Commander."

"I'm afraid I'm under orders to keep you put, miss," the fellow answered. He offered a smile, to soften the disappointing news.

She frowned, thinking on this. "Could you call him in, then? I think it may be important."

The sailor was clearly moved by her alarmed sincerity, but he only glanced down the passage way, and explained with regret, "I've no one to send, miss, and the Commander is above-decks, with the Captain. We can't be interfering with them, when the launch is underway."

With a bit more urgency, she pleaded, "It is very important that I speak to him." She lowered her voice. "I believe my life is in danger."

The man hesitated a moment, weighing his choices, and then nodded. "Right, then; I will escort you up."

And so, Kanika found herself emerging onto the deck, amidst the organized chaos that always took place, whenever a large sailing ship was preparing to weigh anchor.

The Commander stood with the ship's Captain, watching the men as they finished securing the cargo in the hold, and when he spotted her, he strode over immediately. "Take her down below, please," he said to the sailor, in a voice that made no effort to suppress his displeasure. "She's a distraction."

"Pardon me, sir; she wanted to speak with you—said it was important."

"What's this?" asked the Captain, as he joined them. "You've orders to keep her secured below, sailor."

It seemed clear that the sailor was regretting his decision to bring Kanika above-decks, and so she spoke up on his behalf. "Please; do not blame him," she said. "I saw something strange, and I think I must tell you. There is a man aboard—he was a servant, at the Nizam's Palace. It—it makes me wonder if the new Nizam has sent him to do me harm."

The Commander and the Captain exchanged a glance, since this was entirely plausible; if Kanika held the knowledge that the new Nizam was planning to run a secret smuggling operation, then she must not be allowed to travel back to Bengal with the British contingent, when they confronted him about it. And in any event, the extraneous widow was exactly that— extraneous, and no one would give it a moment's thought, if she were to be killed in an "accident."

"Describe him," said the Captain, as he signaled to an officer, to come to his side.

Kanika considered. "He is not Chinese, but he is dark-haired, and dark-eyed. He is not as tall as you, and rather thin."

The Captain glanced over at his officer. "Any new recruits fit that description?"

"Two or three; let me call them in, for questioning."

"Let's shove off, regardless," the Captain decided, a bit impatiently. "We're already a few days behind schedule. We can do the questioning once we're underway."

"If I might make a suggestion," the Commander offered. "In light of recent events, it may be prudent to seize these men immediately."

Kanika kept her gaze lowered, and avoided his eye. *He is wary,* she thought with a hint of amusement; *and he doesn't trust me an inch.*

"A good point," the Captain conceded. "Let's hold off on the launch as long as possible without missing the tide; pull them into my quarters, on the double, and we will hear what they have to say."

"Yes, sir."

And so, a few minutes later, Kanika stood with the Captain and the Commander in the Captain's Quarters, as the first sailor was hauled before them—

understandably nervous, and fingering his cap in his hands.

"Is this the fellow?"

"No," said Kanika, shaking her head, slightly. "This is not the one."

"Next one," the Captain called-out impatiently, and then Hahn was escorted through the door, looking just as nervous as the first sailor.

"You," Kanika accused, her eyes narrowed. "You were at the Nizam's Palace."

Hahn blinked. "What?"

"State your name," barked the Captain.

"My name is Michi, sir."

Kanika had to lower her gaze, and keep it firmly on the floor for a moment, since this was the name of the Reverend's cat.

"You are from Calcutta?"

"No, sir—I am from the Tanka tribe, sir. I did not steal anything—I swear it on the souls of my ancestors."

"Do you know this woman?"

With a show of bewilderment, Hahn glanced at Kanika, and stammered, "No—but I would like to know her, if I should. She is very beautiful."

"You are a liar," Kanika accused.

"You are not at all beautiful, then," Hahn quickly disclaimed.

"Perhaps we should hold him, here," the Commander suggested. "Best take no chances."

"I'll set him ashore," the Captain agreed.

"But—will I be paid?" Hahn ventured, in palpable dismay.

But Hahn was not to hear an answer, to this rather vain hope, because suddenly, a huge explosion rent the air, shaking the ship to its timbers.

CHAPTER 12

"Sound the alarm," shouted the Captain, as they rushed out onto the deck, and Kanika duly noted that the Commander kept a firm grip on her arm, in the process.

As the "all hands" bell rang in the background, the Captain shouted to an officer, "Report!"

"An explosion belowdecks, sir—it looks to be in the aft quarters."

This seemed undeniable, since a billowing cloud of black smoke was pluming out from the area of the ship where Kanika's bag had been stowed in her cabin.

"Form a fire line—get the buckets," the Captain shouted. "I will need to know as soon as possible whether the fire can be contained—otherwise, we'll offload as much of the cargo as we can."

But the Chinese representative on board objected strongly to this plan, since he knew all too well what would happen, if the cargo boxes were to be transferred back to the dock, in the midst of the confusion.

"I can't leave it to be destroyed," the Captain told the man in exasperation;

"Stand aside." He then shouted to his sailors, as the licking flames began to be visible, above the stern's gunwale, "All hands to the fire—form a bucket-line."

"I will send my passenger back to the Compound— I will return," the Commander shouted, over the din, and the Captain managed a distracted nod.

"Come along," the Commander said to Kanika, as he hurried her back down the gangplank, having to squeeze aside, as men rushed the other way to fight the fire. He then called over the men who'd accompanied her litter—the two guards watching the burgeoning fire with no small alarm.

"Take her back to the Compound," the Commander ordered the larger man. "See that she speaks to no one."

"Yes, sir," the man agreed, and quickly moved to open the half-door to the litter.

"You," the Commander said to the other man. "Come with me; we'll be needed."

The other man hurried after the Commander

toward the ship, as Kanika's escort firmly took her arm. "In you go, miss."

Willingly, Kanika ducked into the litter, taking the opportunity to glance over her shoulder at *The Empress*, whose stern now appeared to be entirely engulfed in flames.

Her guard leaned in the doorway. "Let me see your hands, miss—I've orders to check for weapons."

Willingly, Kanika held out her hands, only to gasp in surprise, as he seized both her wrists in one huge hand, and then looped a silken cord around them, quickly pulling it taut, so that her hands were pinioned.

"There is no need for this—I will not try to escape," she protested angrily, but then she began to struggle in earnest, as he efficiently began to lower a sail bag over her head. Furious, she twisted away, and then tried to stand on her feet so as to run, but she was immediately lifted off her feet, and rather roughly hoisted over the man's shoulder, as he jerked the bag's drawstring closed around her feet.

Whilst she continued to struggle, the guard's terse voice said near her ear, "He's given me orders to choke you out, if you don't stay quiet, miss. He doesn't want to do it unless it's necessary, but don't think that I won't."

Thoroughly alarmed, Kanika went still, her gasping

breath loud in the close confines of the canvas bag. Then, with silent speed, Kanika could feel herself carried away.

CHAPTER 13

*I*t was an unexpected development, of course, but she wasn't as alarmed as she should have been, because it seemed clear that the Commander was the one behind this abduction. And—to be truthful—she could hardly fault him; the only flaw in the Reverend's plan was that someone might become suspicious too soon, and it appeared that the Commander had done just that. He may not have known exactly what was planned, but it seemed obvious that he'd been expecting trouble, and therefore had made a contingency plan.

She listened carefully, trying to gauge where she was being taken, but the bag muffled any sounds—not to mention it was close and hot, in the already humid climate, which made it rapidly very uncomfortable.

The man who carried her said once, "Can you

breathe?" and she nodded. Otherwise, he was silent. She could still hear shouting voices, in their immediate area, and decided—rather to her surprise—that they hadn't left the wharf. This conclusion was reaffirmed, when she was lowered—a bit more gently, this time— onto a hard surface, that was rocking, slightly—a boat? —and then she could feel the sudden movement, as the craft pushed off.

Kanika entertained the troubling thought that— perhaps—she was to be dumped into the sea with her hands bound, but then discarded this idea, since it seemed clear that the guard had been instructed to let her know immediately that it was the Commander, who was behind this turn of events. Nevertheless, she silently worked the cord that held her wrists, hoping to free her hands enough to lay fingers on her *katar,* and cut herself free.

She hadn't been successful, by the time she was hoisted-up, yet again, and then the man seemed to balance her on his shoulder as he held her tightly with one arm—up a ladder? She lay still, and strained to listen, but could hear no sounds which would indicate there were others around them, or that they were anywhere near the burning ship. Thankfully, she was soon swung down onto a softer surface, and the bag was unceremoniously pulled from over her head.

Drawing in deep lungfuls of air, Kanika looked

around her. She'd been deposited in a spartan cabin, dim, because there was no window.

"You're to stay quiet," the man cautioned, as he loosened her bonds. "There's a flask of water, there in the corner."

Kanika nodded her understanding. He didn't seem the type to be swayed by a pretty face, and therefore, she decided to take his advice, and ask no questions. It seemed clear she was aboard a boat of some kind—she could feel the slight, rocking movement, and it smelt of the sea.

The man left, closing the cabin's pocket-door behind him, and Kanika weighed her chances of escape. Her hands were no longer bound, and she had her *katar*, but she wasn't certain that an escape was necessarily the wisest course. The marker had fallen in spectacular fashion—leave it to Hahn, to bring it about —and now there would be even more reason for the British to be furious, when they confronted the Nizam. After all, Kanika had raised her suspicions of sabotage just before the explosion, and now it could easily be believed that the India side of the trading-scheme had decided that she should be silenced, at any cost.

And, in light of these facts, it appeared that the Commander had decided to contain her, here— wherever this was—which was probably a wise move, considering her history. After all, he'd promised to keep her safe, and so it could be presumed that she was not in any immediate danger. Therefore, after considering her options, she decided it would be best to remain where she was, and await events.

After several hours, there was a knock on the cabin door, which slid open to reveal the Commander, who looked her over with an assessing glance, as he stepped within.

For her part, she returned his review silently, and without complaint, since she'd learned a long time ago that one shouldn't speak, when one wasn't yet certain what to say.

"I must beg your pardon, if I have caused you alarm—I have taken these measures to ensure your safety. This is an East India Company cutter, and I thought it best to stow you here for the time being, rather than bring you back to the Compound. If this was indeed an assassination attempt, it allows me to observe who shows an interest in your whereabouts."

"Oh—yes; I understand," she replied.

Unspoken was what seemed to be the obvious fact that there would have been no harm in telling her of this plan, instead of bundling her off with a sail bag over her head. Therefore, this seemed a strong indication that that he was not—in truth—so much worried about her safety, as he was worried about whether she was involved in the plot to destroy *The Empress.*

If she were in his place, though, she could hardly blame him. He knew she was not what she seemed, and he must be wary, about bringing this particular blighted bride back to the British Compound, for yet another round of mayhem. And—on the off-chance that she was indeed the target of an assassination plot —it would be best to take no chances that any British personnel would be put in danger.

In the end, it didn't much matter. Hahn might wonder where she was, but the markers were all falling in order, just as they were supposed to, and Hahn would have every confidence that she could see to herself. She would have every confidence, too, save for the fact that she was finding it a powerful experience, to be alone in the cramped cabin with this very capable man, who'd managed to outfox her. He was hatless, and had taken off his coat and cravat, during the fire suppression; therefore—with his damp shirt, clinging to the outlines of his chest—she was getting a fair idea of what he looked like without it. Immediately, she lowered her gaze.

"I must go. I may keep you stowed here tonight, so that I can continue to make note of anyone who shows an interest in you. I'm afraid I can't allow a lamp—we don't want anyone to guess that you are here."

"That does seem wise," she nodded. "Thank you, sir."

Apparently, he wasn't fooled by her demure tone, because he then reached to put a hand under her chin, and lift her face to his. Leaning in, he said, with a touch of humor, "Don't try anything, please. Note that I haven't searched you for weapons."

He was referring to her *katar*, and his kindness in allowing her to keep it, and she couldn't help but smile slightly, as he looked into her eyes. And then, she suddenly realized—*oh; I think he is going to kiss me.* Almost without conscious volition, she pulled away, and he immediately relinquished her chin.

She lowered her gaze, and castigated herself for a fool—it was a rare chance, and it was not as though either one of them was unversed.

There was a small pause, and then he said, in the more formal tones she was used to, "I will return as soon as I am able; please stay below."

She lifted her gaze, and tried to restore their former footing. "You needn't worry, sir; I cannot swim."

"And I cannot believe a word you say to me," he replied, with all good humor, and then ducked his head, as he exited out the cabin.

Kanika took a long drink out of the water flask—she was thirsty, after having been bundled in the bag—and lay down on the bunk. It was close and warm, in the windowless cabin, and she needed to rest—she'd need her wits about her, to navigate the next few days, since it was becoming harder and harder to pretend that she wasn't involved in all the various disasters that were befalling the British opium trade, one after another. Indeed, she surmised that this was half the reason the Commander had stowed her here—not to keep her safe, but to observe what happened once she was out of commission. It was the same as what she would have done, in all fairness.

She found the gentle rocking of the boat very soothing, and didn't realize she'd fallen asleep, until she woke suddenly, not certain of what had awakened her. It was completely dark—so she must have slept for a goodly space of time—and, even more alarming, the cabin seemed to be heeling over, and making a creaking noise; was the ship underway? It was disorienting, in the dark, and she tried to decide whether this was just her imagination.

Trying to tamp down her alarm, she groped until she found the cabin's pocket-door, and felt for the slot that opened it. She pulled at it—half expecting the door to be locked—but found that it easily slid open.

Pausing, she listened for a moment—no need to walk into a trap, after all—and then thought she heard the murmur of men's voices, above; the tenor of the conversation casual, and unalarmed. Cautiously, she tiptoed up the galley-way steps, feeling the immediate relief of the breeze against her skin, as she raised her head above the confines of the galley-way.

Catching her breath in surprise, she paused a moment, to take in the amazing scene that presented itself. The ship was indeed underway, and bounding, a bit, as it moved forward. There were three masts—creaking, in rhythm—with the moonlight glinting off the white canvas sails, as they stretched-out taut against the wind. The ship plowed through the sea that surrounded it—Kanika could see no shoreline, anywhere in sight. It was a cloudless sky, and the stars shone brightly, overhead.

The conversation behind her abruptly stopped, and she could hear a man say quietly, "Best raise him."

Yes, Kanika thought; *best raise him.* She'd more than a few questions, about her present situation—although it seemed apparent that she'd been spirited away, rather than temporarily stashed in the cutter, as she'd been told. Another successful gambit, by the clever Commander.

But she was not one to panic, or even be much alarmed. It seemed clear that she'd little choice in these matters—or at least, little choice, just now—and so she decided that she would very much like to walk to the bow of the cutter, and take a closer look at this wonderful scene, that was filling up all her senses.

The men were standing on a raised area behind her, where the wheel was, and she gave them a long, benign glance—just to show she wasn't panicked—and then she slowly stepped out onto the deck. Carefully, she walked to the fore of the ship, grasping the occasional stay, to steady herself—the ship's movement seemed a bit unpredictable. After coming to the bow, she hung back a bit, clinging to the foremast, and taking-in the sensation of the salt spray, and the more pronounced movement, beneath her feet. Without thinking, she put up a hand, palm first.

The Commander spoke from a few paces behind her. "Exhilarating, isn't it?"

"I am not certain what that means," she admitted, without turning to face him.

"Thrilling," he amended. "Exciting."

She lowered her hand, and frowned, slightly. "No; instead the sound—the hissing, it makes—it is so peaceful."

He stepped a bit closer, and offered, "It isn't always like this. I started out in the navy, and a rough sea is nothing to trifle with."

"Why did you leave?"

There was a small pause. "I was needed elsewhere."

"By evil men," she noted, in a dispassionate tone.

"By men who needed to pay for soldiers," he replied. "So as to put a stop to evil men."

"St. Paul said that the ends should not justify the means."

There was a surprised pause. "I will admit that I did not expect you to cite St. Paul to me."

"I am a Christian."

"Are you? I did have the sense you were laughing at me, when you spoke of your Nairian gods."

She smiled, and lifted her hand again, to spread her fingers. "I would never laugh at you—you are far too serious."

"You may laugh as much as you like, so long as you marry me."

Completely shocked, she turned to stare at him, the movement causing her to stagger a bit, and clutch at the foremast to regain her balance. "*What*?"

"It would be for the best," he continued, as though it was an ordinary topic. "You will need protection, and I am willing to offer mine."

"You are mad," she declared, and quickly turned to face forward, again, so as to control the sudden leap of her pulse.

"And practical. It's going to be a long voyage, and somehow, I have to convince you to let me kiss you."

Neeka, you are such a fool, she thought, and briefly closed her eyes. Aloud, she explained, "It was not—I was—I was just taken by surprise."

"Don't apologize—it was a huge relief, actually. I was entertaining the unwelcome thought that your object, in all of this, was to seduce me. But that is obviously not your aim, or you would have let me have my way with you, when you had a prime opportunity."

She stared ahead, unable to speak, and cursing herself, for a hundred-times fool.

"So; we will marry."

Oh, Neeka Neeka Neeka, she thought, but replied steadily, "We mustn't."

"James," he prompted. "We mustn't, James. And yes, we must." He reached a hand to gently tuck-back a tendril of her hair, that had come loose in the wind.

Quietly, she informed him. "I am betrothed."

She could hear the amusement in his voice. "The Hong has broken off your betrothal, I believe."

"I am betrothed to someone else," she admitted. "In truth."

"Then I will render my apologies to the fellow, if I ever run across him."

She decided that it would be best to change the subject. "Where do we go, that I have such need of your protection? England?"

"No, we sail to Bengal—Calcutta, more precisely. We will visit the Nizam, because I have a few pointed questions to ask of him, and it is important that you be present."

"Oh," she said. "I see."

And there you have it, she thought to herself, rather firmly; *I will be long gone, before any such confrontation could possibly occur.*

CHAPTER 15

*H*er legs idly dangling over the side of the ship, Kanika rested her head on her arms—which were crossed, along the railing—and watched, as the waves rolled off the hull, mesmerized by the sound, and the sensation. She'd found that she could sit, thus, for hours on end, and not mind the inactivity.

How surprised Hahn will be, that I have disappeared, she thought. Although it was more likely that he would relish the challenge—he was never one to be the least bit daunted, when faced with a setback. Not that it was much of a setback, of course. The markers were falling, one by one, even if they were falling in unexpected ways. She would wait until she could consult with Hahn once again, and then they would decide how to best move forward.

With some disquiet, she realized that Hahn would not catch-up to her for some time, after they landed in Calcutta—the Commander had been clever, with his well-thought-out plan. He'd made sure no one knew where she'd gone, before he'd bundled her on a fast ship to her new destination—and not one of the ships that made the usual opium circuit, between Canton and Calcutta, but instead, a sleek, anonymous cutter.

Hahn would eventually find her—he was Hahn, after all—but he'd be days behind, even under the best of circumstances. And in the meantime, the Commander had ensured that the new Nizam would be caught by surprise, when she was hauled before him, and asked to explain what he knew about this particular blighted bride—his aunt-by-marriage—and the blatant attempt to undermine the Company's opium trade.

Which, in turn, accounted for the Commander's unexpected offer of marriage. Women held little importance, amongst the ruling class in Bengal—especially widows, and *especially* widows who held embarrassing secrets; secrets that might jeopardize lucrative trading agreements, with the powerful East India Company. Therefore, the simple solution for the current Nizam would be to immediately place all blame on Kanika, and then have her put to death, without a moment's regret or hesitation.

In fact, even if they were headed instead to her home in Kerala—where women of her caste were given more deference, than the usual—there was nonetheless little doubt that she'd be likewise as quickly sacrificed. With the failed uprising fresh in everyone's minds, no one there would have the fortitude to defend her against the Company, and—in the end—she was merely a woman, and therefore expendable.

And yet, by stark contrast, here was an Englishman, who recognized her danger, and was willing to take action to protect her—even as he suspected she might be plotting his ruin.

It was rather amazing, all in all, and it made Kanika reconsider some of her preconceived notions about who was evil, and who was not—although the Reverend had already made great inroads, in that regard. Of course, it helped that the Commander was attracted to her—that much had been evident, from the first. But for the man to offer marriage seemed to be an almost foolish display of chivalry—even the Reverend had not anticipated such a potential turn of events. Hahn had been willing to marry her, because they were old friends, and allied in their quest to bring down the opium trade, but the Commander would be acting against his own interests.

This thought gave her pause. *Be careful, Neeka,* she

cautioned herself. *His reasons may not be as chivalrous as they appear.*

In the meantime, she found that she was greatly enjoying the voyage—even enjoying the dull routine of the days. There was something to be said, for this feeling of being suspended in time, with nothing but the endless ocean, stretching out in every direction. There was naught to accomplish—even if she held the means to do it—and so she spent a great deal of time in her present position, listening to the hissing of the waves below, and thinking about nothing in particular. *No wonder, Abhay loved the sea, so much,* she thought idly; *I would have gone happily in his place.*

The Commander was polite, but tended to leave her alone, save for their chess matches, in the evenings. The ship's Captain allowed them the use of his cabin— which held a map-table—and they would sit and play together, for an hour or so, after the evening meal.

At first, there was little conversation—mainly because she was wary of his intentions—and she sensed that he recognized this. But gradually, they began to speak more; he was interested in how she'd learned to play, being as in the usual course of things, women in India were not allowed.

"I played with my father, before he died," Kanika explained, thinking there was no harm in telling him. "And then I met a Missionary, in Kerala—at

Tellicherry Fort. He played with me—hours upon hours—and he taught me some of the newer gambits."

"You play very well."

She smiled, because the compliment was sincere, and not at all patronizing. They'd discovered that he was the better player, but that she could at least challenge him, on occasion. Once or twice, he'd suggested that he start the game less a rook, so as to make it more equal, but she liked it better when they held the same advantages, even it if meant that she lost on a regular basis. It helped her to learn.

"How did you manage to stab Sir Jost?"

"I hid in a banyan tree, and I ambushed him," she explained, and moved her knight.

There was a small pause, whilst she could sense his gaze upon her. "That's no easy feat."

"It was before I became a Christian," she admitted, as she studied the board.

"I have the feeling," he said slowly, as he moved his rook, "that you wouldn't hesitate to do it again, and Christianity be damned."

She couldn't help but smile, and acknowledged, "Perhaps. He wanted to rescue me, but I did not wish to be rescued."

"I can understand his dilemma, then."

She raised her gaze to his, and saw the amusement

therein. "I am from a warrior tribe," she explained. "We do not crave safety."

He raised a brow. "If I may say so, your warrior tribe might have done better to crave a small measure of safety."

Fairly, she admitted. "This is true—so many of them were headstrong, like Abhay, and never considered that they might lose their lives, and lose everything, for their families. They wanted only vengeance, and to make the British suffer, as they had suffered."

He bent to study the board again. "That is the exact recipe for how to lose a war. I've witnessed it myself, plenty of times."

"Yes; you would never be so headstrong, and take such risks."

A smile played around his lips. "You'd be surprised."

Sensing that he was about to move the conversation toward his offer of marriage, she just as firmly moved it elsewhere. "Nevertheless, I am grateful that I did not go with the Dutchman, to England; instead, I found my own path."

"With the help of the Missionary."

"Yes." She added, "It was not an easy thing, though. It is hard to forget the old ways—to see the world with new eyes, and try to make sense of the new ways, where there are no castes, and no gods, living in the sacred groves. But he helped to show me how; he spoke of forgiveness, and of the greater good."

"He sounds like an admirable Missionary, then."

Careful, she warned herself, and again, shifted the subject. "Since I am a Christian, now, I am supposed to forgive the British—and forgive the Dutchman, too— but I am not certain such a thing is possible."

"You cannot be blamed, certainly. I struggle with that concept, myself."

This was of interest, and she glanced up at him. "Do you have reason to forgive the Dutchman, too?"

"Not as yet," he said, with a trace of humor. "Although it's early days."

She smiled in response, and moved her queen— who was in danger; she'd not been paying as much attention, as she should. "How do you know him?"

"I was serving aboard a man o' war, in the Battle of Lissa, and he was serving as a Captain, aboard another ship."

"I do not understand anything about what you said," she confessed.

"A sea battle," he explained. "In the war, that I told you about. Thanks mainly to Sir Jost, it was an unexpected victory."

After deciding that here was another topic she

wished to avoid, she laid down her king. "I resign," she announced. "This was not a good night, for me."

"You may try again tomorrow, then," he replied, and rose to open the door for her.

It is very pleasant, she thought, as she passed before him, *to be with a man who does not treat a woman like a child, who must be cajoled and flattered—or be ordered about. He is rather like Hahn, in that respect—although Hahn would be astonished to hear it.*

"Good night, sir," she said. "Thank you for the game."

"It was my pleasure," he replied, and she could feel his gaze on her, even as she walked away.

CHAPTER 16

They'd been sailing for a good space of time —perhaps a month, although Kanika couldn't be certain, since she hadn't thought to keep track of the days, from the beginning. Lately, however, she'd seen a distant shoreline, on occasion, to the starboard side of the craft—the Malay Peninsula, the Commander had told her, when she'd asked him.

During that evening's chess match, he explained, "We will cross the Bay of Bengal, and arrive at Calcutta within the week, barring bad weather."

She made a wry mouth, as she studied the board. "I'd not thought to see Calcutta, again."

"Or the Nizam," he added.

"Or the Nizam," she agreed.

His gaze rested upon her. "I thought you haven't met him, as yet."

"I haven't," she agreed, not at all discomfited, at being caught-out.

He tilted his head. "Yet, wasn't it the Nizam, who arranged for your marriage to the Hong?"

"I am but a pawn, in the plans of rich men," she explained. "There was no reason for the new Nizam to meet with me." For emphasis, she moved her pawn into danger.

He scooped it up, and continued, "He didn't grant you the traditional year's mourning, for his uncle. It is a bit surprising."

With only the barest hesitation, she agreed. "No. He wished me gone, it seems."

"More likely he wished to make a contract with the Hong as soon as possible. He hardly waited until after the old Nizam's funeral."

"Yes; such things do not matter, when it comes to the rich men, and their plans."

With a touch of humor, he replied, "You mustn't paint with such a broad brush; I might be considered a rich man, myself."

Kanika kept her gaze on the board, and shrugged, slightly. "I am told it is better to have little, with righteousness."

He chuckled. "Touché. Your Missionary taught you well."

They played for a few more minutes in silence, and

then he said, "If you could tell me what you know of your betrothal—what you were told—I would be in a stronger position to assist you, when I meet with the Nizam."

Interesting, she thought, and hid her alarm. *He has avoided this subject, but now he is probing, and I imagine it has to do with the fact that we are fast-approaching the moment of truth.*

"I was told only to prepare for the journey, and for my new life, in Canton."

But he only tilted his head—it was becoming familiar to her, the way he politely tilted his head, when he disagreed with whatever had been said. "You are no fool, Kanika. You must have known that your dowry consisted of opium, and that you'd been sent overland, so as to avoid British scrutiny at Canton harbor."

"I am not fond of the British," she reminded him. "I would not have raised any alarm, even if I were given a choice."

"You'd no choice?" His gaze held hers.

Surprised, she met his regard. "No—of course, I'd no choice. I am merely a woman—and a widow, at that. In this world, we are not given choices."

With a sudden intensity, he leaned forward, the game forgotten. "But now, you do have a choice, and I wish you would take it. You are at risk, Kanika, because the Nizam holds authority over you, as your closest male relative. If he can put-off all blame onto you, I imagine that he will not hesitate."

"Yes—I understand," she agreed in a grave tone. "It is very distressing."

He hadn't re-introduced the subject of marriage during the voyage—perhaps hoping she'd soften her attitude—but now—now, with their arrival fast-approaching, it seemed that he'd no choice. It was just as well; she'd been patiently waiting for this conversation, and strategizing how best to handle it.

He continued, "If you married me, I would hold authority over you, instead, and the Nizam would dare not move against me."

"Yes," she agreed, and then added with all gratitude, "It is a very generous offer."

Watching her reaction, he added, "Your betrothed—whoever he is—cannot protect you as well as I can, due to my position within the Company."

With a slight frown, she ventured, "Perhaps I needn't be present, when you speak to the Nizam?"

But he tilted his head, slightly. "It would be best if you were. It has been my experience that the Bengal trading-partners will roundly deny any self-dealing, but with you there, telling your tale, he will be forced to make concessions—especially if I hint that he may have arranged for the death of his uncle, your husband."

She listened and nodded, seeing the wisdom of this.

"But—as it stands—I cannot prevent him from taking you into his custody, and we'd have no grounds to refuse such a move. The last thing we want, in this situation, is to give him an excuse to have his own grievance against the British."

He paused, so as to emphasize the seriousness of the situation. "If he doesn't have you killed outright, for bringing this trouble down upon him, he will arrange for another marriage—one that will bring him advantage. Once again, you'd have no choice."

"Yes," she agreed.

Sensing his advantage, he pressed, "You'd have much more freedom, married to me, than if you were married to just about any other man in the world. You'd make your own choices, always—my promise on it." He paused, and then added, "And if you wish to avoid my bed, that is a choice you can make, too—I'll not press you. You cannot tell anyone, though, because it must appear as though ours is a true marriage."

"Oh, no—no, that is not a concern," she assured him immediately. "You are very—indeed, you are very —" Flustered, she held her hands up to her cheeks. "Oh; you make me blush."

His brow knit, he pressed, "Then, what is your concern? What makes you hesitate?"

Surprised, she pointed out, "But, I am not hesitating, sir. Indeed, I have told you 'yes,' many times already."

There was a small silence, and then he smiled broadly, so that his teeth showed—the first time she'd seen him smile, in such a way. "You won't regret it—my oath on it."

He offered her his hand, across the table, and she took it, catching her breath, when the warmth of his hand closed around hers. "Prepare to blush even more, Kanika. The Captain can marry us tonight, and you will move to my cabin."

Oh, she thought, very much relishing his intent expression, made all the more compelling in the candlelight; *oh—this is truly not fair*. Aloud, she said, "Yet, I would ask for one thing, sir. Instead of the Captain, I would like to be married by a Christian minister, in a Christian church. It is important to me, to honor my new faith."

He thought this over, still holding her hand in his. "That should be no difficulty—there is a minister, stationed at Fort William. It is only important that we be married before the Nizam arrives."

She smiled her appreciation, because it seemed clear that he was so relieved she'd agreed, he was willing to make whatever concessions she desired. It was a strange and novel sensation; she'd married Abhay because their parents had arranged it, and she'd agreed to marry Hahn because the Reverend had arranged it. But this—this was quite different; even though this man recited many practical reasons for wishing to marry her, she knew—in that elemental awareness, that existed between men and women—that he was determined to have her, and was willing to do whatever was needed, in order to achieve this aim.

It was of all things pleasing, and—very much pleased, in turn—she teased, "I will allow you to kiss me, if you still wish to."

"I do wish to," he said immediately, and rose to draw her to her feet. "In truth, I have wanted to kiss you from the first time I saw you."

"It did not seem so," she admitted, a bit breathless from the sensations he engendered, as his hands moved to her arms, and he pulled her close. "You were very serious."

He drew her to him—with one arm around her waist, and the other raised so that he could cup her face in his hand, his eyes intent upon hers. "I was wary. I am used to having beautiful women paraded before me, by men with ulterior purposes."

She lifted her brows, and placed a tentative hand on

his chest. "That is unfair, I think. It was your men, who plucked me out of a tree."

"Well done, on them," he murmured, and lowered his head to kiss her.

She'd been curious, about how it would feel when he kissed her—more than curious, actually; very impatient, more like. But she wasn't prepared for the sensation that overwhelmed her—like a thunderclap, in its strength.

She'd thought to allow him a few chaste kisses—in keeping with her modest demeanor, and their unmarried status—but as soon as his lips touched hers, she found herself aflame, opening her mouth to his, and clinging to his shoulders as though she couldn't press him to her close enough.

And it seemed that he was all too willing to match her fire; in a matter of moments, she was frantically helping him unfasten the ties on her dress—all whilst trying not to disengage their mouths—and then, with the dress lying in a heap on the cabin floor, he lifted her easily, and carried her over to the Captain's bunk, where—once they fell onto it, with their mouths still locked together—her impatient hands pulled at his shirt, so that he willingly broke away for a moment, to lift it over his head.

His eager hands began to divest her of her undergarments, and in the process, his fingers brushed across her *katar*, and then quickly moved away from it. Making a sound of impatience, she pulled the tie on the cloth sheath, herself; foolish man, to think that she'd leave it on, so that it would press into her flesh.

And indeed, her flesh was pressed in ways she'd never imagined, as his weight bore down upon her, and she welcomed their coupling without hesitation or thought—it was not a time for thinking, for once, and she found that she could only relish the respite.

CHAPTER 17

*I*t is not such a terrible thing, Kanika argued to herself, as she stood on the deck, and watched, as the sailors dropped anchor in the Bay of Bengal. *After all, the Reverend himself said we must remain flexible, in the event that any markers were missed, so as to regroup, and recalibrate.*

Not that they'd missed a marker, but it had definitely become more complicated, then what was originally planned. Who would have thought that the man would offer marriage, as protection from the Nizam, or that she'd be whisked away from Hahn, so that she was forced to improvise on her own, and without his counsel?

Making a wry mouth, she admitted to herself that it was providential, that Hahn was not here, on this voyage. If he were, she'd never have behaved like a wanton with the Commander, for the past few nights. Who knew, that sexual congress could be so very—so very *pleasing*? It had not been her experience with Abhay. Truly, it quite filled one's mind.

As though on cue, the Commander glanced her way, from where he stood beside the Captain near the rail, and she couldn't help but smile, at the remembrance she saw in his eyes.

Neeka, Neeka, Neeka, she scolded herself; *don't forget what is at stake, and try to curb your lust.*

The Commander turned to approach her. "Good morning," he said, that warmth still present, in his eyes.

"Good morning," she replied in a demure tone, and resisted an impulse to giggle—she was a grown woman, after all.

"I will arrange to have you escorted to the Women's Quarters, at Fort William, and we will be married day after next, if that is agreeable to you."

"Very much so," she willingly replied.

He bent his head to hers for a moment. "It would be best, I think, not to mention our plans. The Nizam has his spies, and we don't want anyone to guess that we plan to marry, so as to stay his hand."

She nodded. "Yes, I understand."

Gently, he prompted, "James."

"James," she agreed, and then explained, "It is not something I am used to—to call a man by his name."

"I know. I do like to hear you say it, though."

"Then I must learn."

But he shook his head, slightly. "You will do as you wish, Kanika. I'll not force you to be someone other than who you are."

"Then you must have a care," she teased. "I am a Kshatriya of Nair—I come from a long line of warriors."

"You may wage war or not, then, with my blessing. I would only ask that you don't wage it on me."

This teasing remark hit a little too close to home, and to cover a pang of dismay, she reached to lay a hand on his arm—another thing, that she was unused to.

He covered her hand, briefly. "I am afraid they will throw a dinner party for me, tonight, at the Government House. You may attend or not attend, as you wish."

She blinked in surprise. "Women will be allowed to attend this dinner party?"

"They will. It is our custom."

This was interesting, and she weighed her choices, before deciding, "I would like to attend, then. I must learn how to behave like the English."

"I can find no fault whatsoever with the way you behave," he replied in a warm tone, and again, she suppressed an inappropriate urge to giggle.

The sailors began to lower the tender-boat from its davits, and he touched his hat. "I will see you tonight, then. Don't forget; say nothing about the wedding."

"I won't," she agreed. She then watched him walk over to where the sailors were unfurling the rope ladder into the tender-boat, as he stopped to speak to the Captain. *He is happy*, she realized. *He is one who hides his emotions—like me—but you can see his happiness, in the way that he walks, and in the set of his shoulders. He is happy, because he believes he has found happiness in me.*

She closed her eyes, briefly—very much dismayed by the pang of sadness, that this thought engendered. *Stay strong*, she urged herself; *what you do for him will be many times better, than if you indeed married him.*

The sailors assisted her down the rope ladder, and into the rocking tender-boat—the smaller boat more suited for the short voyage up the River Hooghly, to the Calcutta docks, which were located inland. She hadn't a hat—having been abducted from the Canton docks without warning—and so, one of the sailors held an umbrella aloft, so as to shield her from the still, hot sun. It was a strange experience—to be in the small boat, with a group of polite Englishmen—and so she kept her gaze firmly on the shoreline, as she sat in the stern. The Captain and the Commander spoke of the Captain's next port-of-call, as the sailors rowed in unison, without once glancing up at the beautiful woman seated facing them, with her head uncovered, and her long hair unbound.

They know I belong to the Commander, she thought, *and they don't dare engage with me.* With some surprise, she realized they must think her a concubine, and it was an unsettling thought—women of her caste did not become concubines. *I am not supposed to be prideful, anymore,* she reminded herself, *I am supposed to be humble—and make whatever sacrifices are necessary, for the greater good.*

This, of course, was easier to accept when the Reverend spoke of it, than when she found herself in a boat-full of Englishmen who thought her a concubine, but she lifted her chin, and calmed herself; she mustn't allow the Commander to think she was not as docile as she pretended—although, to be honest, he seemed to know very well that she was not as docile as she pretended, and this fact did not seem to concern him in the least.

Don't think about that, she warned herself. *Think instead of what lies ahead.*

Unfortunately, what lay ahead necessarily included another visit to the damp and airless tombs, and she could not anticipate such a thing with any enthusiasm. *Humility*, she reminded herself firmly, and watched, as the shore drew ever closer.

CHAPTER 18

At the dinner-party that evening, Kanika sat beside the Lieutenant-Colonel's wife, and listened politely. The older woman was extraordinarily pleased with herself, and naturally assumed that Kanika would be so, too.

Upon her arrival at Fort Williams, Kanika had been assigned a maidservant, who saw her bathed and thankfully dressed in new clothing—another western gown, purchased from the Fort's Commissary. The young woman—Millie—seemed remarkably incurious, about Kanika's arrival at the Fort with no baggage, and she sought no explanation as to how it had come about. Kanika, therefore, drew her own conclusions, and didn't attempt to engage the maid in conversation; instead, she carefully watched the other woman's actions, without appearing to do so.

At the appointed time, Millie escorted her to the Government House, where the banquet for the Commander was being held, and Kanika found herself seated at a table adjacent to the head table, as it seemed no one was quite certain where she fit in, with respect to the military institution's careful hierarchy. Indeed, Kanika was rather surprised to note that the English appeared to have their very own caste system, as she listened to the prattling woman who sat beside her.

"We were quite astonished, when Commander Colton arrived with no advance notice, but no one can throw a party together like the Governor-General's wife." Kanika's companion nodded her head toward the dignified, elderly woman who was seated to the right of the Commander. "Her husband's the Company's ranking officer, here in India, and he's paid a tidy sum, as a result—plenty of pin-money, for her, even though there's not much to spend it on, in this God-forsaken place."

"I suppose this is true," Kanika ventured, not certain how to respond.

Perhaps realizing that she'd offered insult, her companion offered, "You see a different side of the place, of course—they say you're some sort of nobility, around here. One of the old Nizam's wives." Her eyes held a calculating expression, which Kanika interpreted as weighing how much deference should be given to someone who was a noblewoman, albeit from a God-forsaken country.

"Yes, that is correct," Kanika replied, with a small smile.

The woman shook her head slightly, as she re-addressed her meal. "You should be wearing widow's weeds, then—I don't know what your maid was thinking, to purchase light colors."

"Oh—I hope I do not offend," Kanika offered.

"No—no; you poor thing, you couldn't know better." The woman patted her hand in a kindly manner, before declaring, "It is impossible to find decent servants, here."

Kanika could make no complaint, however, because she'd managed to convince Millie that—aside from a gown suitable for the banquet—she would need a new *sari*, also. She'd explained to the young woman that she would have need of the traditional Indian garment, if she was scheduled to meet with the Nizam—he would think it very strange, if she were to appear before the head of her family, in western dress.

Her dinner companion seemed to have decided that perhaps the beautiful stranger seated beside her might have something of interest to say—or at least, something that could be passed on, since it appeared that the older woman excelled in gossip. After casting a calculating eye at Kanika, she ventured, "My husband tells me there was a terrible fire, at the wharves in Canton, and that you barely escaped."

"Indeed," said Kanika, in her softest voice. "It was very frightening, and I am grateful to Commander Colton, for rescuing me."

Raising a brow, the woman looked upon Kanika in an amused, arch manner. "Well, if you are thinking of casting your handkerchief his way, think again. He's not one to be beguiled, even by as pretty a one as you."

"Oh, no—you mistake," Kanika disclaimed. "I cast no handkerchiefs." She then looked to her plate, struggling to hide her amusement.

"Well, it wouldn't be a surprise, is all—there's plenty who do." She nodded toward the head table, in a knowing manner. "The Lieutenant-General's daughter, for one."

Thus directed, Kanika followed her gaze to the pretty blonde, who was seated at the Commander's right hand.

"She shouldn't be seated there, of course, but her father's pushing it—so very obvious, but he doesn't care. Although she's got two thousand a year, so it might well be tempting, for him."

"That would be a great advantage," Kanika noted politely, and felt a stab of sympathy, for the Commander. He'd said that he was well-used to dealing with such ploys, by men with ulterior purposes, but it must be an annoyance, nonetheless.

Her thoughtful gaze was then caught by one of the servants, who was waiting on the head table—not really a servant, per se, since this was a military installation; instead foot soldiers had been enlisted, to serve the guests. The servant bent to retrieve a fork from the floor, and then said something near the Commander's ear that went unacknowledged; very unusual, for the ever-polite English, and particularly so, for the ever-polite Commander.

Her attention was then drawn back to Kanika, as the woman concluded, "We'll wait and see—he's a hard nut to crack. They say his heart's in the grave."

Kanika admitted, "I am not certain what this means."

"He's a widower—his wife died." She ate another forkful, and added, as an aside, "The wife had five thousand a year—easily—as well as a tie-in to the Montagus."

"Oh; I see," said Kanika, with a show of being duly impressed.

Reminded, the older woman eyed Kanika sidelong. "I hear rumor that you're worth a pretty penny, yourself."

"Not as much as five thousand," Kanika demurred.

"Well, my husband says you're to be delivered back

to the Nizam." Kindly, the woman paused, and patted Kanika's arm again. "It is just as well, dear; he'll find you another husband. Better luck, next time."

"I would be most grateful to him," Kanika agreed, and then listened with a sympathetic air to her companion, as they addressed their dessert—it appeared the woman had a rival, in the Lieutenant-General's wife, and wished Kanika to hear her of her many grievances.

Not really listening to her companion—who was perfectly content to hear herself speak, after all—Kanika allowed her gaze to wander over to the head table, and saw that the pretty Lieutenant-General's daughter was chatting vivaciously with the Commander, who listened with a polite expression, but glanced over his companion's head, toward Kanika. Their gazes met, for the barest instant, and then Kanika lowered hers, again.

A shame—that we are both constrained by manners, she thought. *He chafes at this sort of thing, as much as I do, and we'd both rather be back on the cutter, playing chess. Or abed.*

Scolding herself for allowing her thoughts to wander, Kanika returned her polite attention to the woman seated beside her, and made a sound of sympathy.

CHAPTER 19

Kanika stood in her second-story room at the Women's Quarters, and slid a finger between the curtains, to surreptitiously review the scene in the assembly-yard, below. Her maidservant—Millie—had gone to fetch wash-water, but Kanika thought mid-morning seemed an odd time to go to fetch wash-water.

There; the woman was returning, a jug hoisted on her shoulder, and Kanika was not very surprised to see that she walked with the soldier who'd waited on the Commander, last night—the man who'd retrieved the fork.

Kanika stood back, and watched, until the two of them walked beneath the window, and out-of-sight.

When Millie returned with the water, she fished around in her apron pocket for a note. "I was asked to give you this—it's from the Commander, ma'am."

Kanika smiled, and shrugged her shoulders, slightly. "I am afraid I do not read English."

"Oh—would you like me to read it to you, then?"

"Yes, please."

Millie unfolded the parchment, and squinted a bit, as she concentrated on the script. *I have arranged for the Nizam to visit, day after next. To discuss these events, I will call upon you tomorrow morning at 10 am, if I may.*"

Millie looked up. "It is signed by the Commander."

With a show of dismay, Kanika stood, and began to pace the floor. "Oh—I am to be given over to the Nizam, and I do not think he will treat me well. It is most distressing."

"They can't blame you, that it turned out to be such a disaster," the maidservant offered, as cold comfort. "And the Nizam's just as much to blame, for sending you over there, all secret-like."

"Yes—it is so very unfair," Kanika exclaimed, in an agitated manner, and duly noted that Millie seemed very well-informed.

Suddenly, Kanika turned to the other woman, and took her hands with a beseeching gesture. "You must help me—please. I fear the Nizam means to kill me."

"Surely not," the woman soothed, as she carefully withdrew her hands. "You're his kin, after all."

But Kanika shook her head. "Not to this Nizam—I was merely his uncle's fourth wife. I am wealthy, and he seeks my riches; he will insist on *suttee*—it is the way of my people."

Frowning, the woman fingered her apron. "I don't know what's to be done, ma'am."

But Kanika pleaded in a low tone, "I can escape; I know of people who will hide me, at the sea port. You must know the fishmongers, here—I need only someone who has a boat, to take me downriver, to the Bay."

For an instant, Kanika discerned a calculating gleam in the other's eyes, before the young woman admitted, "Why, yes—yes, I do." She paused, and then added, as though inspired, "My—my sweetheart's a fisherman, as a matter of fact. Jem—yes, Jem's his name."

Not a very good liar, Kanika thought, but smiled with tearful relief, at the other woman. "Oh—oh, that is *perfect*. He can take me to my friends—they will hide me where no one will be able to find me."

"Will they, indeed?" asked the maid, whose working-class accent slipped, for a moment.

"They will pay him—my friends will pay your sweetheart," Kanika assured her. "Two gold coins, if he will take me to them, and tell no one."

The maid studied her for a moment, her own face

expressionless, and Kanika could see that she was trying to decide the best course of action. Therefore, she added, "I must escape, whether he helps me or not; he may as well be the one who is paid for it."

With a decisive nod, the girl agreed, "I'll ask him, then."

"Tell no one," Kanika cautioned, in a serious tone. "It is worth my life."

"I won't," the girl promised, and quickly moved toward the door, forgetting that she should curtesy, first.

An hour later, Millie returned to report that all had been arranged. "I don't want to get into trouble," the girl explained, "and so we'll go for an evening walk, along the maidan by the riverfront, and I'll tell them you slipped away from me. I'll look for you for a half-hour, before I raise the alarm."

Listening intently, Kanika nodded. "How will I know your sweetheart's boat?"

"It is a blue boat, and he will tie a red rag, to the mast."

With an emotional smile, Kanika bowed her head in gratitude. "Oh; oh—thank you. I owe you my life."

"I'm glad to help you, ma'am, and Jem is glad for the money."

Kanika nodded, and turned toward her bed. "I must lie down, now, and rest."

"I'll bring your dinner later, and that's when we can go for our walk."

"Thank you again, with my whole heart."

After the maid closed the door behind her, Kanika walked over to the wardrobe, and pulled her *sari*, from within. She changed her garb, carefully folding the western dress, so as to place it beneath the straw mattress. She was arranging her headdress to cover her hair, when she heard a quiet knock at the door.

Oh—no, no, no, she thought in alarm, and quickly yanked the western dress from its hiding place, and scrambled to pull it back over her head. Smoothing the skirts with her hands, she assumed a serene expression, and answered the door.

Millie stood on the threshold, holding a vase filled with flowers, and—almost to her surprise—Kanika suffered a stab of acute disappointment, that it wasn't the Commander. The maid said, "These were left for you below, ma'am; I thought I'd bring them up, before I left."

"Thank you, Millie."

The maid placed the flowers on the bedside table, before remembering to dip a curtsey, this time, and then leaving yet again.

Kanika blew out a breath. It had been foolish—to think that the Commander would come upstairs in the

Woman's Quarters, so as to visit her. And it was doubly foolish, to be so disappointed that he hadn't.

Unable to resist, she walked over to examine the bouquet—because that was what it was, of course; a bouquet of local flowers, tied together with a ribbon, and resting in a vase of water. There was little doubt that this was intended to be her wedding bouquet, for the morrow.

Neeka, she cautioned herself, as she touched a lily petal with her finger. *Remember who you are, and stay strong. But oh—how it chafes, to think that I am just another beautiful woman who was paraded before him, by a man with an ulterior purpose.*

Straightening up, she rejected the comparison; the Reverend was selfless—a rarity, in her experience—and he was genuinely attempting to serve the greater good. The unassuming Christian Missionary had concocted a bold plan to save the world, and—amazingly enough —it was working; it was working very well.

I will explain it all to the Commander—I will write him a letter, she promised herself. *Somehow, I will do it; he deserves that much—he has always treated me with such respect, and I must return the courtesy. We understand each other, and so, he will understand this, too.*

Having come to this resolution, she felt somewhat better, and quickly pulled the western dress off over her head, once again, and re-donned her headdress.

I won't tell Hahn, or the Reverend, but I will write the Commander a letter, she thought, as she secreted the western dress beneath the mattress again. *I will apologize—no, not apologize, because I cannot be sorry. Instead, I will give him my reasons, and my regrets that it had to be this way. Perhaps I will send him a katar, like mine, so that he may remember me.*

Quickly, she suppressed the memory of the Commander, examining her dagger in his hands, as he lay beside her in the narrow bunk, and asking her what it meant—the *shikra*, on its hilt, and the traditions it represented.

It was a bit too painful, and so—rather than dwell on the fact she'd likely never see him again—instead, she lifted the water jug, and watched out the window until the courtyard was clear—it was early afternoon, and few were going about their business, in the hot sun.

Dropping the jug onto the dirt below, she slid over the window sill after it, finding a foothold on the casement for the first-floor window, below hers. Scaling quickly down to the ground, she immediately straightened up, balanced the jug atop her head, and then began walking to the nearest gate, in an unhurried manner.

With her veil drawn modestly across her face, she walked through the fort's main gate with an air of complete unconcern. Then, once she was well-away, she abandoned the jug behind a tree, and began to slide from shadow to shadow, tree to tree, heading upriver—the opposite way she'd told Millie—and toward the ancient graveyard that lay next to the River Hooghly.

CHAPTER 20

"I didn't think I'd see you again, Miss," the woman offered, as she lifted the flask of water from its hiding place, in her flower basket. "Did you burn yourself, this time?"

"No." Kanika smiled, and turned over her fingers. "Your salve worked well—thank you."

Under cover of darkness, Kanika had quietly made her way to the graveyard that was adjacent to St. John's Church, here in Calcutta. She'd hidden here once before, after the Nizam's Palace had burned down. Deep within the crowded array of moss-covered tombs, an unassuming mausoleum served as a hiding place for runaway slaves—or the occasional woman, who'd managed to escape a *suttee*. The Pastor of the church asked no questions, and no names were ever exchanged, but anyone seeking refuge would be quietly transported away, by sympathetic parties. The Reverend had known of it—even though he'd never been to Calcutta—and he'd explained to Kanika that many of the Christian churches in India cooperated in operating a secret refugee network—one that helped runaway slaves, in particular.

The woman—thin, and work-worn, was the caretaker for the tombs in the churchyard, and she would smuggle food and clothes to the runaways in her flower basket, as she ostensibly tended the graves.

Kanika gratefully watched, as the caretaker unloaded bread and cheese, wrapped in a light cloth. "Any place you're looking to go? Or just away?" Fortunately, there were ships always anchored in the Bay of Bengal, from many parts of the world; indeed, it was the main reason that the refugee network had a station, here in Calcutta.

"I am not certain how long I will need to stay," Kanika explained. "A man is coming to fetch me, and he will know to find me here."

"Very well," the woman replied. "Do you need clothes?"

Kanika nodded. "A sailor's kit, would be helpful."

"I will see to it."

"Many thanks."

She left, and Kanika grimaced, as she crawled into the recesses of the mausoleum, and then groped in the darkness for the straw pallet, that lay in the corner. It would be important not to emerge, for a few days, but she was not looking forward to another stay, here—the mausoleum was necessarily dark, and airless. After the Nizam's fire, she and Hahn had hidden here for a few days, making the final preparations before they'd set out on their river journey to Canton. She didn't have fond memories of this place; she chafed at inactivity, and hated to feel constrained.

With stoic resignation, she tried not to think about how it had felt aboard the cutter, with the endless horizon stretching out before her, and instead lay down to sleep. She'd stayed in a cave, once, under similar circumstances, and a bit of hardship was a small price to pay, for the goal that was—finally—within reach.

The Commander may have disrupted the plan, when he'd stolen her away from Canton, but all in all, they'd achieved a great deal, and with more to come. Amazing, what could be accomplished, if one were bold enough—it was just as the Reverend had predicted. All would be well; she'd only to wait for Hahn, and then they'd adjust the plan, so as to determine the next marker, in light of the obvious fact that the Commander seemed to be well-aware that she was no ordinary bride, caught-up in these strange and tumultuous events.

With a mental shake, she tried to erase the image of

the caretaker's basket of flowers. She'd had to look away from it, because it reminded her, rather painfully, of the Commander's bouquet, and how she'd been scheduled to be—for once—an ordinary bride, on the morrow.

Impatient with herself and her wayward thoughts, she turned over, trying to find a comfortable position— no easy task, on a straw pallet. By now, he'd know that she was gone—the sly maidservant would have reported that their plan to thwart her escape had been thwarted, in turn. He'd be unhappy, of course.

Do not think about him, she commanded herself sternly.

This proved a difficult task, and so she soothed the emotions that roiled within her breast by assuring herself, once again, that she would write to him—write and explain. No one else need know, but she felt that she owed it to him—they'd had some wonderful nights, on the ship.

Don't think about that, either, she commanded herself quickly.

And so, Kanika spent the next two days in semi-darkness, during the day, emerging only to walk the tombs, under cover of night. *Hurry, Hahn*, she thought, and tried to make a realistic guess at when he'd arrive; after all, he'd have to first figure-out what had happened, and that may take a few days, in itself.

Then, he'd have to sign-on to the next ship bound for Calcutta—he didn't dare try to pose as anything other than a common sailor. The ship wouldn't have the speed of the cutter she'd sailed—it would be laden with cargo. And so, a few more days delay.

At least a week, she decided, with stoic resignation. *He's probably at least a week behind me, but if it's any consolation, I know that he's chafing at it, just as much as I am.*

Therefore, it was with extreme surprise that Kanika heard the caretaker's voice call out to her that evening, just as she'd laid down, to sleep another tedious night away.

"Miss," the woman whispered. "He's come to fetch you."

With an enormous burst of relief—leave it to Hahn, to beat all expectations—Kanika scrambled to the tomb's entrance, only to pause in astonishment. It was not Hahn, who stood behind the caretaker, but the Commander.

CHAPTER 21

With mixed emotions, Kanika stared at him, almost unable to believe the evidence of her own eyes.

"Don't run," he said. "I'd only find you again."

Recovering her voice, she pleaded, "You mustn't bring harm to these people. Please."

"I won't. Come outside, and let us discuss what is to be done."

There was something in his voice that made her say, in a rush, "I am truly sorry. I was going to write to you, to explain—I swear it."

"No need, now."

She duly noted that the constraint had left his voice, and then she chastised herself for her weakness, in trying to ease his feelings. She hadn't been able to help it, though; all along, she'd had to fight an almost overwhelming urge to trust the man. She didn't dare, of course; he was who he was, and she must fight this powerful feeling—this feeling of having an allegiance to him, despite everything.

She swallowed. "Are you alone?"

"I am. Come outside; I don't relish sitting in a tomb." He turned to the caretaker. "That will be all, thank you."

But the caretaker—a slight woman, with no more strength than a butterfly—looked to Kanika. "Miss?"

"Yes, it is all right. He is not who I expected, is all."

The other woman turned to walk away, and the silence stretched out for a moment, as Kanika and the Commander regarded each other. "Would you like to walk, or sit?"

"I would like to walk," Kanika confessed. "Mainly, I would like to walk to the river, and bathe."

"Then let's go," he replied, and they set out, necessarily walking a bit slowly, amongst the dark, uneven shapes of the tombs.

She thought she may as well ask. "How did you find me?" Astonishing, that it had been so swiftly done, and it made her uneasy—perhaps this graveyard wasn't the safe haven that the Christian network thought it was.

He offered his hand, so that she could step over a broken, moss-covered statue. "What they do here is an open secret, amongst the British naval officers. Many of the people who are hidden here wind up on Company boats, bound for other ports."

She frowned at him in suspicion. "How can this be? The East India Company supports slavery."

"The East India Company doesn't support anything, save making money," he replied a bit dryly, as he steered her through a narrow passage, between two tombs. "To this end, it rarely interferes, in the social customs of others." He glanced over at her. "The British people, however, do not condone slavery—quite the opposite, in fact."

But she observed, in a curt tone, "You make a distinction that does not exist, in this part of the world. The East India Company is all we know of the British."

He nodded. "I will grant you that. But even this part of the world is changing, Kanika—and for the better, I believe. And the main reason it is changing, is because traders are trading, and spreading new ideas." He still held her hand, and he squeezed it, slightly, for emphasis. "St. Paul understood this, better than anyone—traders, traveling to new ports, can bear great influence."

Mulishly, she withdrew her hand from his, and countered, "Traders care only for making money—you just said so, yourself."

"It is why they explore, and go to new places," he

agreed. "You will have a hard time finding any man on earth, who doesn't wish to better his family's fortunes."

"You have no such excuse—you have no family," she retorted.

There was a moment's pause. "I will. It is why I am here."

The quiet words inspired an almost suffocating conflict of emotions, within her breast, and she suddenly confessed, "Forgive me; I am unkind to you, because I am glad you came, and I shouldn't be."

"I know," he said, and took her hand again.

They walked in silence to the river's edge, and Kanika raised her face to the slight breeze, savoring it, along with the sounds of the evening that could be heard along the river—the night insects, and the occasional loud voice, as the fishermen called to each other, on their way home. She should be planning her next move—deciding how to behave with him, so as to protect the plan—but she couldn't seem to think. It was as though her mind had lost all its ability to function, the moment she'd beheld him, standing outside the moss-covered tomb.

"Shall I hold your clothes?"

"Oh—oh, would you? I would so very much like to swim, and wash the scent of this place from me."

He tilted his head. "I thought you couldn't swim."

"It was not the truth," she admitted, as she pulled her sailor's tunic over her head.

"Don't swim away," he cautioned.

"I won't—I will give you my *katar*, as a pledge."

But he'd removed his hat, to set it on the ground, and he began unbuttoning his coat. "Better if I stay within arm's length."

She smiled, bemused. "Indeed, you will swim in the Ganges?"

He shrugged out of his shirt. "Isn't this the Hooghly?"

Casting an appreciative eye over his bare chest, she explained, "The Hooghly is the Ganges. The waters are all the same—and they are sacred, to us."

"Don't tell your Missionary you said as much."

She smiled, as she turned to step into the cool water, he close behind her. "He was always careful not to criticize native beliefs."

"Rather like the East India Company, then."

Giving him a look, she replied, "You will not change my mind, on this subject." She then submerged up to her shoulders, and sighed a happy sigh.

"Fair enough."

He submerged completely under the surface, and then came up, to shake the water from his head with a practiced movement.

"You are like a dog," she teased.

"Oh, I've had many a navy-bath," he replied, and ran his hands through his hair, so as to smooth it down. "Only we always had a sentry, posted with a musket, to set the sharks."

Idly, she moved her arms in the cool water, and asked, "What does this mean?"

"There are sharks in the ocean—dangerous, great fish, who would like very much to make a meal of a man."

"I know this," she agreed. "The ocean in Kerala has sharks, too."

"They are not very smart, the sharks; if you shoot one of them, the others will go into a frenzy, and attack each other. They will leave the men alone, even though the men would be the easier prey." He paused. "So, we always had a man ready to set the sharks, if any showed up."

"And this works?" she asked in surprise.

"It works very well. We only lost one or two men, every voyage."

She stared at him in astonishment, and he chuckled, as he reached to draw her to him. "I am teasing you, Kanika."

"I don't think I could swim in the ocean, if there were sharks—even with the man watching," she confessed.

"Oh, I've no doubt you'd acquit yourself well," he

replied, and she laughed, and suddenly, it felt how it had felt those last few days on the ship, when they had been so very attuned to each other.

He held her afloat, as he idly walked along the river bottom, with the slow current swirling around them, and the eternal stars of India, reflecting off the water. With her wet skin pressed close against his, it seemed as though every sense was in harmony with the world around them—the night, the water, and the smell of the rich earth. *Here is a memory I shall never forget*, she thought, even as she lived it.

The interlude came to an end all too quickly, and he steered them back toward the riverbank. He hadn't mentioned what was planned, and she decided that he'd avoided the subject long enough. Therefore, to broach these matters, she ventured, "I am glad you came. But I am not certain it was for the best."

He helped pull the sailor's shirt back over her head —no easy task, since she was still damp. "You will be the better for it, that much I can promise. Who do you wait for, here?"

As he shrugged back into his coat, Kanika weighed what to say, in light of the fact he obviously knew more than he was saying. "My betrothed," she admitted.

He nodded, as though this was in accordance with what he'd suspected. "I see. I will have to offer-up my apologies to him; we need to be married, and as quickly as possible. To this end, I have enlisted the Pastor, here."

Taking her hand, he began to walk toward the church, its dim outline rising in the near distance. "This way, please."

CHAPTER 22

Thoroughly astonished, Kanika stared at him, even as he led her away. "You—you cannot be serious."

He tilted his head, slightly. "I am always serious—you said so, yourself."

"But—you make no sense; I ran away from you—you cannot trust me."

"I am a stubborn man, Kanika."

Her thoughts in wild disarray, she continued to stare at him as he led her up the slight hill to the church. "I am not with child," she ventured.

"It doesn't matter; you have need of protection, and I will offer mine. Come along."

Utterly bemused, she fell into step alongside him, as he walked in a determined manner toward the church, its dark structure rising up before them, silhouetted against the lighter sky.

In a rush, she confessed, "It is not a good thing—that you are so stubborn. You mustn't marry me; it is a trap."

He cocked his head toward her. "How would our marriage be a trap?"

"I cannot tell you. Be thankful, that I give you warning—I shouldn't."

Thoughtfully, he walked a few steps in silence. "I think it could work."

Exasperated, she exclaimed, "Are you listening? I am trying to ruin your life."

"James," he prompted. "I am trying to ruin your life, James."

"James," she agreed, and couldn't help but smile, despite her exasperation. "I am trying to ruin your life, James."

"You are going to ruin my life, either way. I may as well gain some enjoyment from it."

They were fast-approaching the church door, and Kanika suddenly realized that she'd no desire whatsoever to resist this—this enlistment. With a touch of panic, she warned, "You won't deter me, you know. And then your life will indeed be ruined, as you try to explain your foolishness. You are loyal to your goals, but I am loyal to mine." She added, after a moment's hesitation, "James."

He pulled open the heavy wooden door, which was unlocked. "What is your goal? To disrupt the opium trade? You won't succeed; it is making too many people rich, including the farmers, here in Bengal."

"And the British," she added, with a touch of bitterness.

"The East India Company," he reminded her. "Recall that they are not one and the same, no matter how it seems, here."

"You are their hero," she accused, trying to convince herself to flee.

But he only replied, "They won't be happy with me about this, certainly. Feel free to take a measure of solace, in that thought."

And then, they were approached by the Pastor, who gave off the impression that it was wholly routine, to be conducting a secret, night-time marriage ceremony, with two people still dripping with water from the river.

"Are we ready?" he asked, in a mild tone.

"We are," the Commander replied.

There was a still, small silence. "Yes," Kanika agreed.

CHAPTER 23

*A*nd so, with no further ado, Kanika found herself being ushered before the altar, blinking a bit, in the light of the single candle that adorned it.

The Commander took her hand, and—with the caretaker as witness—the Pastor opened his Book of Common Prayer, and began to recite the ceremony.

Hahn will be amazed, that I managed this, she thought; *but he will never know that I am the reluctant one, here. I shouldn't be—I should be rejoicing, that this man was so easily duped. But I know him better than Hahn does—and he is not one to be easily duped; it makes me worry that I am the one, who is being duped.*

"Please face each other, for the vows," the Pastor said.

The Commander took her hand, and repeated the

Pastor's words, his voice echoing slightly, in the dark and deserted church. He seemed rather grave, as he gazed into her eyes—perhaps he was remembering this same ceremony, with his first wife. Kanika, of course, could make no such comparison with her own first wedding, since this ceremony seemed absurdly short. Her wedding to Abhay had gone on for days, and—as was the tradition—didn't allow for much participation, by the young bride.

It was now her turn, to say her vows, and she tried to match the Commander's tone, as she repeated the words—stumbling a bit, over his middle name—Matherson—which was difficult for her to pronounce.

And then, it was over, and the Pastor was presenting them with the marriage lines, to sign.

The Commander stepped closer to the candle, so as to carefully review the document, and then—apparently satisfied—he folded it within his breast pocket. "Thank you," he said, and handed the clergyman a discreet envelope, which was quickly tucked into the man's waistcoat.

"My best wishes, Mrs. Colton," the man said to Kanika, and bowed.

"Oh. Oh, thank you," said Kanika. It was very strange; in Kerala, a woman did not take her husband's name.

They walked out of the church, and then stood

alone for a moment, outside on the steps, as the night insects chirped in the background, and Kanika tried to decide if it had all been a dream—it almost seemed so, in a strange way.

"We will stay in the Pastor's guest room tonight," the Commander said, taking her hand. "I'll not miss my wedding night, and he must be able to affirm that the marriage was consummated, in the event it is ever questioned."

Unable to resist a smile, she admitted, "I have no objection, to this."

He smiled in response, and then bent his head to kiss her. She willingly kissed him back—it was as he had said; if he was going to ruin her life, she may at least obtain some pleasure, from it.

He tucked her hand in his arm, and they began the walk toward the Rectory. "Tomorrow, we will return to Fort William. I think it would be best if you are returned to the Women's Quarters, and that we say nothing of our marriage, as yet. When I confront the Nizam, I would prefer that he not be aware you have my protection—not at first, anyway."

This was rather surprising—that he felt it necessary to gauge what the Nizam planned, before disclosing their marriage—but since Kanika didn't plan on being present for the visit from the Nizam in the first place, she simply nodded in agreement. "As you wish."

He chuckled. "You alarm me, when you are meek, and obedient."

"You alarm me in turn, when you do not wish to tell me of your plans."

She glanced up at him, sidelong, and he squeezed her against him, with a show of regretful acknowledgment. "I am sorry for it, but there are competing considerations, and I must try to find the best way forward. In the meantime, I would ask that you trust me."

"It appears I have little choice," she said lightly.

He opened the Rectory door. "It appears I have little choice, James."

"James," she willingly amended.

Pulling her close to his side, he murmured as they mounted the stairs. "Let's see how many times I can make you call out my name."

Unable to help it, she giggled.

CHAPTER 24

Kanika lay, drowsy and content, in the Commander's arms. He was making up for lost time, it seemed, and to be honest, so was she; it had been a very hard thing, to think that she may never have seen him again—may never have experienced this bliss, again.

Remember your purpose, she sternly reminded herself. *You mustn't be distracted.* She then acknowledged to herself that she would be very much surprised if—no matter how resolute she was—the Commander did not manage to track her down again, even if she fled to the ends of the earth. Since this thought engendered diverse emotions within her breast, she decided not to dwell upon it.

She could sense her companion's sudden tension—he stilled, as though listening—and then she heard what he'd heard; a quiet, creaking sound, as the window-sash was raised.

In an instant, he'd rolled out of the bed, and stood at the ready, his pistol in his hand. "Don't move," he commanded. "Explain yourself."

Slowly, Hahn stood upright, his hands spread, and his figure silhouetted by the moonlight that streamed in through the open window.

"Don't shoot," Kanika cautioned, gathering-up the bed linens, so as to cover her naked breasts. "I know him."

"*Neeka*?" Hahn whispered, in bewildered astonishment.

There was a moment's silence, as Hahn's gaze traveled back to the Commander, standing naked, with his pistol. "This is indeed awkward," he ventured.

"He is my betrothed," Kanika explained to the Commander.

"Then I must beg your pardon," the Commander said sincerely. "But the lady is now my wife."

"Yes," Hahn replied slowly. "I can see this."

In a rush of remorse, Kanika told him, "I am so very sorry, Hahn, but it was for the best."

In hurt amazement, Hahn slowly shook his head. "I came to fetch you home, Neeka."

The Commander gestured with the pistol. "Again,

my apologies, sir; but it is probably best that you return home alone."

"Neeka? This is what you wish?"

"Yes. I am truly sorry, Hahn. Please give your family my apologies—Drishith, and Karthav." Drishith and Karthav were members of his family who'd been killed in the British suppression, and it was her way of assuring him that all was well, with the Reverend's plan.

With a solemn face, Hahn nodded. "I will. Many blessings, Neeka."

"Thank you."

With all appearance of regret, Hahn turned and exited out the window—making another small, creaking sound, which was very unlike his usual silent ways—and then he shimmied down to the ground, below.

The Commander stood at the window, holding the curtain aside, as he watched Hahn disappear into the night. "So; it was he you were waiting for, in the tombs."

"Yes; word had been sent to him, to fetch me home."

She froze, suddenly remembering that the Commander had seen Hahn in his guise as a sailor, aboard *The Empress.* It was very unlikely that the man who stood before her hadn't recognized him—and so, she quickly tried to think of a plausible story, as to why he'd been there.

But the question wasn't asked, as instead the Commander reached to firmly shut the window. "He is Nairian, also?"

She decided there was no harm in telling him. "Yes. We have known each other from childhood."

The Commander crossed the room to deposit his pistol on the nightstand again, his head slightly atilt. "Interesting, that you remained betrothed to this man, even though you'd married the Nizam, and then you were on your way to marry the *Hong*."

There was a small silence. "Hahn is from my tribe," she explained, in an even tone. "It was agreed that if I were ever left alone, he would see to me."

It was a lame explanation, and there wasn't the smallest chance that her companion would believe it, but he only reached to take her hand, and crouch down beside the bed, so as to look into her eyes. "From here on out, I will be the one to see to you."

Relieved that he wasn't going to press, she smiled. Thank you—James."

But she felt a twinge of uneasiness, as she welcomed him back into the bed, and nestled happily into his side. It seemed to her that the Commander hadn't asked near enough questions—indeed, he'd never even asked for Hahn's name.

CHAPTER 25

And so, once again, Kanika found herself in the Woman's Quarters at Fort William—a surprising turn of events, but nothing that could not be remedied, of course. This time, she'd a guard, posted outside the window, and a different maidservant to attend to her—a brisk, formidable woman who said little, but who'd obviously been warned to be wary. Kanika couldn't help but smile to herself, thinking of the unpleasant Millie, who'd been stripped of her position for being so easily duped.

Kanika was polite with her new maidservant, but made no attempt at conversation. Instead, she gratefully accepted a fresh dress, and then covertly watched through her window, awaiting events.

She wasn't to wait long; the maidservant was summoned below, and then returned to hand her a note. "There's a soldier below, with a message from Commander Colton."

"I cannot read English," Kanika admitted. "Would you read it to me?"

"Certainly, ma'am." The woman walked over to the window, and reviewed the lines of writing. "He says I'm to see to it that you're given a suitable *sari*, and then I'm to escort you over to the Company's offices. The Nizam is on his way, and he's very eager to welcome you home."

Bending her head in a saddened manner that was very uncharacteristic for her, Kanika said with some constraint, "I can only hope that this is true, but I fear the Nizam does not mean well by me."

"Chin up, miss," the woman said, in a perfunctory manner. "Best you go back to your people."

My people were largely wiped out by your people, Kanika thought, but only nodded in a resigned fashion. And so, a few minutes later, Kanika emerged from the Women's Quarters—escorted by her maid, and the soldier—and began the walk across the dusty yard to the Commissary.

"She's a pretty one," the guard said to the maid, in a conversational manner.

"She speaks English," the maid warned.

"Does she? I've given it away, then—I'm sure she'd no idea that she was pretty." The soldier flashed Kanika an insolent grin, which she roundly ignored.

"Enough of that—she's not for the likes of you," the maid informed him, in repressive tones.

"Oh?" the guard teased. "You don't think she'd be willing to make a switch?"

"You're to mind yourself," the maid replied, but could not repress a small smile, and who could blame her? The guard had a very charming manner.

"You haven't read enough fairy stories," the man insisted, laughter in his voice. "I could win the girl, we'd sail away, and then live happily ever after—I could be a fisherman, and she could help me tend my nets."

"I think you've read a good deal too many fairy stories," the maid retorted, but with good humor. "Here's the shop; we shouldn't be long."

Once in the Commissary, Kanika looked over the *saris* that were stacked neatly upon a shelf, and then rather clumsily knocked the pile to the floor. "Oh—oh, I am so sorry."

"No matter, miss," said the shopkeeper, as she crouched down to assist Kanika and the maid, in retrieving the pile. "Here—let me help you."

Once the merchandise was restored to its place, Kanika fingered the offerings, and then chose a likely *sari*—silk, shot with gold thread—as well as a scarf that she could fashion into a headdress.

"Best get dressed," her companion said, as she checked the watch that was pinned to her blouse. "We don't want to be late, if the Nizam is on his way."

"Will you help me change?" Kanika asked, in a helpless fashion. "I am not used to managing alone."

"Certainly, ma'am—although I'm not sure that I'll be much help, when it comes to a *sari*," said the maid, who then walked with Kanika toward the dressing room, located in the back of the shop.

But Kanika paused, as though suddenly remembering, and addressed the shopkeeper. "Have you any parasols?"

"I do, ma'am," the shopkeeper affirmed, and then led Kanika to the display stand toward the front of the store, where the muffled sounds of a brief struggle in the dressing room would be less noticeable.

"This one—thank you," Kanika said with a smile, and then retreated once more toward the dressing room.

She closed the curtain behind her, and quickly turned to Hahn, who was efficiently stripping the maidservant's clothes, from the now-unconscious woman. With his help, Kanika donned the woman's dress, and then tucked her long hair up, under the borrowed cap.

With a last look at her, Hahn nodded in approval, and then he stepped from the curtained alcove to make his way to the front counter, where he began a determined flirtation with the shopkeeper, as he signed the voucher document for the clothes.

For her part, Kanika stepped out from the curtains, and then opened-up the parasol just as she stepped past the shopkeeper, so as to shield her face—not that the girl was paying much attention; she didn't seem to notice that two women had entered, but only one had left.

Walking slowly, in the manner of an older woman, Kanika wielded the parasol to shield her face to any passersby, as she exited the Fort yet again, and walked in a leisurely manner across the maidan, and toward the river. Several small *teppas* were tied up along the dock—small, log catamarans that were used by the locals for fishing. Kanika dawdled until she saw what she was expecting; Hahn, no longer dressed as a soldier, but now in fisherman's garb, striding toward a *teppa*, and then untying the ropes, so as to cast off.

Taking a quick glance around, Kanika stepped aboard, just as the boat drifted away from the dock, and then quickly ducked out of sight beneath its canopy.

CHAPTER 26

Kanika crouched under the canopy on the *teppa*, and was laughing as Hahn explained, "I am sorry that it took longer than it should have. She thought me so very handsome, that I feared for my virtue."

"You are a good catch, and with a steady job," Kanika teased. "And she'd probably rather be married, than minding the shop."

They were in great spirits, as they tended to be, when they'd managed a difficult task successfully.

"You are a magician, Hahn," Kanika continued. "I was worried that you had been delayed at Canton, and that I was indeed going to be hauled before the Nizam."

"You seem to have matters well in hand." This, said with a great deal of meaning.

"Yes," she admitted without shame. "The Commander tracked me down, and then insisted that I marry him. I am sorry to have pulled such a surprise, but it seemed the best thing to do, so as to allay his suspicions."

Hahn frowned slightly, as he cast his line out, and watched it sink into the muddy water. "Do you think he recognized me, from *The Empress*? I wasn't certain whether to confront you."

She admitted, "We should assume that he did—he's not one to forget a face."

"Oh? But he said nothing?"

"No. But he was curious as to how I remained betrothed to you, despite my marriage to the Nizam, and my betrothal to the Hong."

Hahn nodded, in fair acknowledgment, as he contemplated the water's surface. "That is indeed a very good question."

"He is very shrewd, Hahn," she warned. "He should not be underestimated."

"No; definitely not. How did he manage to find you?" He glanced at her, curious.

"They know of the hiding place, in the tombs—or, at least, the Company's sea captains know of it. He said they take the runaways aboard their ships, and ask no questions."

Hahn raised his brows, as he turned to contemplate his line again. "Do they? That is surprising."

"Yes—I thought so, too. He said the British do not approve of slavery—or *suttee*."

"They are a strange people, then, considering what they do approve of."

She made a wry mouth. "Yes, they are a very strange people, and no better example than when he insisted that I marry him, even though I have caused him so much trouble. It seems he fears what will happen to me, when I am returned to the Nizam."

Hahn grinned, as he glanced back at her. "It is you, who are the magician, Neeka."

She admitted, "I have an advantage; it was exactly as the Reverend predicted—the Commander is an Englishman, and he believes me to be a woman in danger."

Bemused, Hahn shook his head. "They are a strange breed of men, to be so concerned over a woman who is not their own. Although I suppose he thinks the Nizam will call for a *suttee* within an hour of laying eyes on you."

But his words reminded her of a troubling thought that she'd held, ever since the Commander had first insisted that they be married—all the way back on the cutter—and thinking on it, she said slowly, "It—it does not make much sense, though, does it? He behaves as though he is powerless against the Nizam, but he is not; in fact, he is more powerful than the Nizam—and can demand whatever he wishes, one would think. Indeed, that is the very reason he was the Reverend's target—he is so very powerful, in the trade."

Hahn listened thoughtfully, and made no comment.

With a knit brow, she continued, "I don't understand it, Hahn; he pretends to fear the Nizam, but instead, it is the Nizam, who should fear him. The Nizam cannot afford to anger the East India Company —we know what happens to the native leaders who do." Troubled, Kanika looked out over the water. "So; why did he marry me, and in such haste?"

"He feels sorry for you?" Hahn speculated. "He wishes to make certain you are not assassinated, in secret?"

But slowly, Kanika shook her head. "Why take such a drastic step, then? It was not necessary that he marry me, to throw his protection over me. And—if that is indeed his reasoning—then why does he wish no one to know of it? Why would he wish to keep his marriage a secret?"

Hahn raised his brows in surprise. "He wishes to keep it a secret? I will say that it didn't look very secret, in the bedroom."

"Well, no," she admitted, and hoped she wasn't blushing. "He said the Pastor must know that the marriage was consummated, and not a sham. But he asked me to tell no one at the Fort—not until he hears what the Nizam will say. Why would this be, though? The Commander is very powerful, within the Company, and it seems strange—that one such as he would wish to move so quickly, and so secretly. Indeed, it should be the opposite; if he truly wished to protect me, he should let everyone know that I am his wife, now. There would be no shame to it, after all—I am a prized bride."

Hahn cocked his head, and duly noted, "Your husbands don't have the best luck, Neeka."

She smiled at the jest, but insisted, "All the more reason not to marry me in such haste."

Hahn shrugged, and then lifted his line, so as to cast it out again. "Maybe he likes you. You are very likeable."

"I am Kshatriya," she reminded him, teasing. "I am too exalted, to be likeable."

Smiling slightly, her companion replied, "Well, he is too exalted to be likable, also. Maybe he sees a kindred spirit."

Hahn was teasing, but this was actually the theory she'd used to argue against herself, even as she knew the Commander's actions did not seem to make sense. It would be so pleasing, to believe that he'd recognized his mate, in her—recognized how very alike they were—and so he was determined to bind her to him, and this was why he was moving so forcefully. But she knew, in her heart of hearts, that there was something else at play. He liked her—and it was true, that they were very much alike—but this did not explain his outsized desire to marry her as quickly as possible, and with all secrecy. Why? After all, the Company would be pleased, one would think, to have an outright claim to her opium fields.

Hard on this thought, Hahn suggested, "He wants your opium fields?"

"Perhaps," she agreed. "But then, why the secrecy? I think there is something here that we do not understand."

With a grin, Hahn pointed out, "Well, it doesn't matter, because there is something here that he does not understand."

Reminded, she said to him, "I think we have little choice, Hahn, but to skip ahead, to the last marker, at Ghazipur. The Commander is very clever, and we should not tempt fate. And we do not dare delay, and take the chance that he will indeed bring me before the new Nizam—if that happens, then all of our other markers would have been for naught."

He nodded in agreement, even as he sighed with regret. "It is a shame. The Records House marker is so close by, and I had such a good plan."

Trust Hahn, to want to tempt his luck; the Company's archives were kept in a small building within Fort Williams, and that building's destruction would obliterate all the Company's contracts with its trading partners. It was indeed tempting, but she only advised, "I will tell you something that the Commander told me, Hahn; sometimes a plan must be abandoned as unwise, no matter how much your heart is set upon it. I think this is one of those times."

"Very true; and anyway, my plan for Ghazipur is equally as good," he consoled himself.

Smiling, she teased, "It should be; Ghazipur should be more than enough, to set the sharks against each other."

Hearing her amusement, he smiled, as he idly tugged on his line. "Tell me what this means."

Willingly, she related, "The Commander used to be a soldier on the ships, for the British. He said when the men swam in the ocean, one of them would stay on the deck with a musket, and watch for sharks. If one shark was wounded, the others would attack it, rather than attack the men."

But she found that Hahn's expression had suddenly turned very serious, as he slowly turned toward her. "Neeka," he said, quietly. "He knows. He knows of the Reverend's plan."

In some surprise, she protested, "No—oh, no, Hahn. I am certain that he does not."

But he only continued, "Think on it, Neeka; we are setting the sharks against each other, you and I. He was testing you, with his story, and you did not see it."

Frowning, she thought about this, but only shook her head. "No. It is a coincidence, only—we were speaking of swimming in the ocean. I'd no sense that he was—that he was testing me." She then looked up at him, sure of herself. "And he knows nothing of the Reverend. I have made certain—I haven't even given his name."

Hahn nodded, and turned back to his task. "Good. Because if he knows—and if he reveals to the others that they are only being provoked, so as to turn against each other—the plan will not work."

"I am certain he does not know, Hahn," she assured him, yet again. "And remember, he thinks I am in danger, and has married me, to protect me. If he'd guessed the plan, he would not have done so."

Hahn's brow cleared, much relieved. "Yes—of course. This is true."

Relieved in turn, she ceased, "You frightened me, for a moment; the Commander is good at chess, but he is not that good."

Hahn nodded. "Nevertheless, it is all the more reason to skip to the last marker, in Ghazipur. Once we destroy the factory, and I plant the evidence, it should be more than enough for all sides to lose trust in each other."

"Yes," she agreed wholeheartedly. "And at the very least, the trade will be disrupted for years, so that there will be no more famines." Reminded, she frowned, slightly. "The Commander told me something, Hahn—he told me the opium must pay for a war, that the British are fighting. He said their enemy is evil, and more powerful than the British. They must pay for foreign soldiers, to fight their war."

Hahn regarded her thoughtfully. "Does that matter? The British are the enemy."

"Not the Reverend," she reminded him. "Do you think the Reverend knows, of this British war?"

Hahn shrugged. "The Reverend is not interested in the excuses rich men give, for becoming richer."

Almost reluctantly, she nodded. "This is true."

Watching her, he continued, "For our people, it is more important that the famine come to an end, than that the British win their war."

She lowered her gaze, feeling a bit ashamed. "I know—I know. I was only surprised to hear—to hear this explanation."

Hahn regarded her for a thoughtful moment. "Maybe he is more likeable, than I thought."

Trust Hahn, to say it aloud—he knew her so very

well. "I shouldn't like him," she admitted. "He is the enemy. I just don't want him to be destroyed, in all this."

Gently, he pointed out, "He would not be destroyed, Neeka—remember what the Reverend said. Instead, it would be the best for him—to be forced out of this evil trade. He may not like it, but it would serve him well, in the end."

"Yes, of course—it is just as the Reverend said." Ruefully, she glanced up at him. "You must think me foolish."

But instead, Hahn said, very seriously, "We will agree, you and I, that if his life is put in danger, then we will see to it that he escapes. The Reverend need not know."

Touched by the promise, she nodded. "You are a good man, Hahn."

"That is because I find you likable, myself," he replied, and turned to resume his fishing.

CHAPTER 27

Ghazipur was located upriver from Calcutta, and the ancient city—rich in history—happened to be located at a strategic spot on the Ganges River, very near the fertile fields of Padua. Therefore, it had long been the logical place to offload the harvests from those fields onto barges, to be sent downriver to the markets of Calcutta. The East India Company—once it had taken over the opium industry in India—had seized this advantage, and had set-up a factory in Ghazipur, to process the opium plants into a dried extract—easily packed in large quantities—to be then sent via river barges to Calcutta. There, the dried opium balls were auctioned off by the Company, so as to maintain the fiction that the Company was not directly importing opium into China—and the merchandise would be sent off to Canton, via the cooperation of the Cohong.

Since Ghazipur was a fair distance up the river from Calcutta, it would have been an arduous journey —and traveling upriver was never easy, considering the powerful tides. Indeed, it would have taken weeks, in the small fishing boat, and so it was fortunate that this was not the plan at all; instead, Kanika and Hahn positioned their fishing boat near the docks of Calcutta, watching and waiting for the latest Company barge to arrive from Ghazipur.

A production schedule had been set-up—efficient and practical, as all British projects tended to be—so that regularly scheduled barges came downriver from Ghazipur, offloaded their cargo, and then returned to the factory for the next load.

Hahn and Kanika planned to make their way to Ghazipur by traveling on one of the returning barges; it was not an uncommon occurrence, since often the barge-masters would be paid for river passage, as a means of making extra money.

But, as they waited several long days for the next barge's arrival, Kanika found herself in an uncertain mood. It did not help matters that she was hot, dusty, and thoroughly tired of having to hide under the small boat's canopy, but mainly, she entertained the certain conviction that the Commander was sparing no effort to track her down, yet again, and she found that this conviction was much more gratifying than it should have been.

To make up for her conflicting emotions, she complained to Hahn, who patiently listened, as he pretended to fish. "Where is the barge? This is bad luck, that we have to wait so long, here. The Commander is not going to give up so easily, and we give him too much time, to find us. It makes me very uneasy."

Hahn looked out over the busy port, as he considered her words. "Then perhaps you should not go upriver with me, Neeka. Perhaps you should make your way toward the sea, and lead him away from the final marker."

Unaccountably annoyed by this very reasonable suggestion, she retorted, "No. We are supposed to work as a team—that is what the Reverend said." Mainly, the Reverend had explained they should stay together, since if one of them was detained for any reason—a realistic fear—then the other could run a distraction, so as to aid in the escape. The Reverend was a very clever man.

"The Commander caught you so easily, the last time," Hahn pointed out. "Perhaps we should not take the chance that he will do so, again. He seems very stubborn."

Kanika took a breath, and tempered her response—Hahn did not deserve the edge of her tongue, after all they'd been through together. "Yes. But I may be fearful for no reason; he'll not be looking for us here, Hahn. Even if he realizes we escaped the Fort by boat, he'll assume we are headed downriver, toward the Bay of Bengal. It would only make sense, since we could lose ourselves in the crowds at the Port."

"Not you," he corrected her gently. "You are not so easily overlooked."

This, of course, was undeniable, and her beauty was the very reason the Reverend had cultivated her, in the first place.

Frowning, she considered his words, and then admitted to herself that he had a very good point. "I should not be so stubborn, that I jeopardize the final marker—we have come so far."

It seemed clear that Hahn had already come to this conclusion, even as he allowed her to make the decision for herself. He reminded her gently, "It is as the Commander said; sometimes we must abandon a plan, even though our heart is set on it. Instead, you could surface somewhere downriver, so as to been seen —quickly, though; it must not look deliberate. Such a feint would lead him away from me, and from Ghazipur."

It was an excellent reminder that Hahn was a

shrewd man, himself, and Kanika nodded, her mood much improved. "I will do it. Although I will regret not seeing the last of the fires."

"I will paint you a picture of it," he teased, and then paused for a significant moment. "If you return to Kerala."

"I will return to Kerala," she promised, rather firmly.

He cast his line out, and reminded her, "You are married to him. He can send you wherever he wishes."

"He won't though, Hahn. We respect each other."

He was silent, and—sensing his skepticism—she added, "It is hard to explain, but it is true. He will not try to force me to do anything other than what I wish."

Hahn glanced at her. "It is as the Reverend said, then; he is a rare man."

Quickly, she assured him, "There can be no future, between us. I will not be a part of this—this evil trade, and he is at the reins of it."

"Perhaps you can persuade him to stop—you are very persuasive, Neeka."

She smiled at the compliment, but confessed, "He doesn't like to do what he does—he has already admitted this, to me. But he believes he is saving his country."

Slowly, Hahn nodded. "I see. As do you."

"As do I."

He glanced back at her, and met her eyes. "I am sorry for it, Neeka."

Brushing off her feelings of sadness, she mustered up a smile. "We are accustomed to making sacrifices, you and I. We will return to Kerala, the Reverend will help me set aside this marriage, and—if you will still have me—we will marry, instead."

"I like this plan," Hahn said, as he turned back to his fishing. "I am sick of being aboard this boat."

CHAPTER 28

*W*rapped in a *sari*—and with a headscarf, pinned across her lower face—Kanika walked in a sedate pace along the bank of the river, where other women were doing their washing. Hahn had bribed a riverman to smuggle her downstream, and now she'd emerged—safely away from Hahn—with the object to be seen for a brief time near the Adi Ganga river mouth, before disappearing, again. To this end, she'd decided to mingle at the market, here, mainly because there were British soldiers, posted to keep order—it was not very far from Fort William.

Assessing the busy activity before her, she chose a likely vendor, and then casually unpinned her veil, so as to approach his stall, only to discover that her tactics were completely unnecessary.

"Promise me, that you won't leap into the river."

Startled, she looked up to see that the Commander had fallen into step beside her, which was as alarming as it was gratifying—it seemed clear that she'd been watched, and from a time far before this.

It is not so very terrible, she argued to herself, even as her heart leapt in her breast; she hadn't planned on being caught—only seen—but on the other hand, she could still steer him away from Hahn, and away from the final marker. To this end, she feigned dismay. "Please—oh, *please,* let me go."

He gave her a look, and said in a level tone, "Where is your cohort?"

She gave up her role as the fearful maiden—he was not fooled, it seemed—and instead she answered, with a show of annoyance, "He has abandoned me."

Instead of replying, he gave her another look.

She sighed, and then offered reasonably, "You must see that I won't tell you."

He gestured for her to walk beside him, away from the busy market. "You must see that I won't tell you, James."

"James," she amended.

"I wish you would; he is in grave danger."

Now it was her turn, to give him a look. "You may think what you wish; I have no fears for him."

"I do fear for him, and with good reason. Let's go back to Fort William, and sort this out."

"I will only escape, again," she warned, in all seriousness.

"Perhaps I can persuade you not to, Kanika."

He looked up, as though deciding which direction to go, and then indicated a frontage pathway that ran along the river bank, where many of the market merchants had docked their boats. Because the market was winding down, the pathway was fairly deserted, at the present time. "Let's walk along the strand, here, where it is quieter."

She agreed, mainly because she didn't want word to get back to Hahn that she'd been taken against her will—he might abandon the last marker, and come to rescue her, instead; despite her bravado, it seemed very unlikely that she'd be allowed to escape a third time, from the confines of Fort William.

Hard on this thought, her companion began rather bluntly, "I would ask that you trust me, Kanika. You— and your cohort—are a threat to some very important British interests, and there are those who feel they must be ruthless, because so much is at stake."

In a gentle tone, she reminded him, "You forget, James, that I am well-familiar, with the Company's ruthlessness."

"I do not speak of the Company."

This was of interest, and frowning, she glanced up at him. "Who do you speak of, then?"

Instead of answering, he said, rather gravely, "You are embroiled in something that is much larger than you realize. It will not turn out well for you, and therefore it is very important that you stay with me—please, Kanika; do not flee, again. I am not certain anyone can keep you safe, but at this point, I believe I have the best chance."

With some confusion, she ventured, "There are those more powerful than you?" This was surprising; the Reverend had made it clear that the Commander was to be their target, due to his important position, and his considerable talents.

"That remains to be seen. It is very important that you do not deny our marriage—promise me, that you won't."

His words reminded her of what she'd planned to say to him, when next they met, and so she steeled herself to say them. "I have been thinking about this—about our marriage, and about you, and me. In Kerala, we have a word for it, we call it *shaapit*—a tainted fate. We are *shaapit*, James."

But it seemed he disagreed with this assessment, as he countered in a firm tone, "No; we do not have a tainted fate. It was the luckiest day of my life, the day I laid eyes on you."

Gently, she pointed out, "But you are loyal to yours, and I am loyal to mine."

"We will find a way, Kanika. My oath on it."

She decided not to argue, and they walked in silence for a few moments, the breeze from the river very pleasant, and the scent of jasmine, heavy in the air. *I should keep this carefully in my memory*, she thought a bit sadly, *for that time when I am without him, again.*

But it seemed he was not inclined to give up his concerns quite so easily. "What is your object, in all this?"

With a show of gentle exasperation, she replied, "I have told you that I will not speak of it, James."

He nodded. "Very well; I will tell you what I think. I think your object is to destroy the opium trade. There have been several strategic fires, which the Company has put down to sabotage, by raiders. Now, I am not so certain that this was the case."

She was silent, and surprisingly unalarmed. She'd already had the sense that he'd guessed the plan—or at least, its broad outlines—mainly based on the way he hadn't confronted Hahn, when he'd had the chance. *He is trying to spare me*, she thought, and felt a pang that she wasn't trying to spare him—not at all. *It is for the best*, she reminded herself. *For him, and for everyone; I must think of the greater good.*

Bending, so that his head was close to hers, he

continued in an intent tone, "It is not such a simple matter, Kanika. Too many men—farmers, with families—depend upon the opium trade, and you cannot make the cure harder than the disease. Will you burn their fields down? There will be a gap in time, before crops can be grown again, and many will starve."

"Many are starving, now," she pointed out, unable to temper the rather sharp retort.

"Only because the farmers choose to take the Company's payments, for the opium crop."

"The Company gives them little choice."

"I will disagree; the last thing the Company wants is an uprising. No one is being forced, against their will."

Pressing her lips firmly together, she was silent, because there was little more to be said; he had his object, and she had hers. It was *shaapit,* and she'd been foolish to argue with him—to even to give him a glimpse, of the Reverend's plan.

And his next words brought this home, as he asked, "Who sent you? Is it the Missionary you mentioned—the one at Tellicherry Fort? Is he part of a larger network, of some sort?"

Kanika hid her alarm, cursed her own foolishness, and repeated quietly, "I will not speak of it, James."

He lifted his head for a moment, and looked out, over the river. "I think he has been a huge influence, on you—your voice changes, when you speak of him. I am waiting for the day it changes that same way, when you speak of me."

She said nothing, as they walked along the quiet river bank, and wondered why everything that had seemed so simple had turned out to be so very, very complicated.

He warned, "You wouldn't want to put him at risk, too."

Alarmed, her gaze flew to his. "You mustn't—he is a good man," she insisted. "He thinks opium is the tool of the devil. He thinks if things continue as they are, wars will be fought over it, with many lives lost."

Her companion took a long breath. "I imagine he has the right of it, unfortunately. And I will readily admit that it is not a simple thing, to know what is best." He glanced at her. "On the other hand, no one is being forced to take opium."

Angrily, she retorted, "But whether they choose to take it or not, everyone starves, because of it."

He bent his head, thinking, as they walked a few more paces—it was what endeared him to her the most, that he always listened to her, so respectfully. "I cannot argue. The Company does attempt to find a balance—we are not as evil as you might think."

With quiet certainty, she replied, "The Company

does not care, that they cause a famine; it only makes it all the easier to control the Indian people."

This seemed to sting, and with some exasperation, he returned, "Acquit me of trying to murder your people, Kanika. If I could help you in your aim, I would, but this is not the way to go about it. You risk your life."

"I am Nairian," she pointed out. "We were born to risk our lives."

"And your numbers are dwindling, because of it."

It was her turn to be stung, and—with an effort—she bit back a hostile retort, and instead offered in a more temperate tone, "Not all of us are like Abhay, and so reckless. Some of us try to make better choices."

"Yes; you were willing to marry me," he replied, and she had the impression he was trying to lighten his tone, because he regretted his unkind remark. "Although that may count as a reckless act, too."

With all sincerity, she told him, "My voice does change, when I speak of you, James. You do not know this, because you are not present, when I do."

This was—after all—the truth; Hahn had known almost immediately that she'd been drawn to the British Commander—against every instinct, and every consideration. And it spoke to Hahn's loyalty that he'd never once berated her, for her foolishness.

"I've never met anyone like you, Kanika. You are completely unafraid."

Willing to change the subject—there was little point in continuing to argue about the last one, after all—she ventured, "Are all Englishwomen so meek, then?"

He nodded. "For the most part."

"The Lieutenant-General's daughter did not seem so," she teased.

He smiled, slightly. "I would very much enjoy this flash of jealousy, if I thought for one moment that you were actually jealous. Instead, I think you know that you may be wholly certain of me."

"That may not be wise, James," she ventured.

"On the contrary."

She sighed. "You are so stubborn—you know that I do not mean well, by you."

He lifted his head, to review the path ahead. "Strangely enough, that doesn't matter—not at all. I am enjoying the challenge, mainly because you are in love with me, and don't dare admit it."

This was plain-speaking, and—since it was completely true—she chose to remain silent. *Shaapit*, she thought, so as to console herself, and try to quell the roiling emotions within her breast. *It is fate, and therefore, it cannot be helped.*

As though aware that he'd unsettled her, he retreated from the topic, and instead continued in a conversational tone, "Is your Missionary married? Was that why you'd gained the impression that Englishwomen were meek?"

Kanika admitted, "Yes—but it is not fair, in a way; his wife was not so very meek, to follow him to strange places, and support him, in his mission."

"There are different measures of courage," he agreed. "Some not as obvious as others."

"Yes—this is true," she said thoughtfully. "And sometimes—like the Missionary's wife—the courage is in serving the greater good, despite the hardship, and the lack of attention. They had a daughter—the Missionary, and his wife; Carena, was her name. She was very beautiful, and impatient with the life that her parents had chosen. And so, she went to England, and married an English lord. He died, but she stayed in London, and lived a shameful existence. She became a rich man's concubine, and it grieved her parents very much."

With an arched brow, he acknowledged, "I'm afraid there are more than a few women of that stripe, in London."

Curious, she raised her face to his. "Oh? Did you have a concubine, in London?"

"I did not. I was a widower."

"Then, all the more reason," she observed, in a practical manner.

"Not for me."

Gently, she probed, "Did you love your wife very much? Can you speak of her?"

There was a small pause, and at first, she thought he'd refuse, but then he bent his head, and began.

CHAPTER 29

"My wife was the youngest daughter of a Baronet, and so my family very much approved of our marriage." He then paused, and seemed to be choosing his words carefully. "She was— she was rather fragile, and did not enjoy being stationed at Canton; she missed England, and longed to go home."

Kanika listened with sympathy, having heard pieces of this story from the Reverend; the Commander's wife had been a quiet woman— intellectual, and ill-fitted for the uncertainty and intrigues that abounded in the small British outpost, halfway across the world.

He continued, "She miscarried, twice, and it made her despondent." He paused. "And so, she began to take opium."

Thoroughly astonished, Kanika stopped dead in her tracks, to stare at him. "*No*," she breathed.

He turned to face her, and nodded his confirmation. "I would confront her, and she would promise that she would stop—with tears and heartfelt apologies—but it only made her go to greater lengths, to conceal her habit."

Kanika nodded sadly, since she'd seen this behavior, herself, and more than once; the Reverend had called opium the tool of the devil, because the addicted could worship nothing else.

The daylight was beginning to fade, as they stood together on the river bank, and the Commander gazed out over the water, for a moment, before he continued, "I finally sent her back to London, to a treatment house, so as to wean her from the drug—it was too readily available in Canton. The doctors there pronounced her cured, and so she was slated to return, and join me again. But—once she was released—she set out almost immediately to visit an opium den, in London. There she overdosed, and died."

Horrified, Kanika was compelled to lay a hand upon his arm, in sympathy. "Oh, James; I am so sorry."

He covered her hand with his own, and bent his head, for a moment. "I will admit I was not devastated, when I learned that she had died—and the shame is mine; she was my wife." He drew his fingers along her hand, and added, "Although I don't know what would have happened, had I still been married, when I met you."

She gently squeezed his arm. "I know what would have happened—you would have stayed loyal to your wife."

He took a long breath. "Perhaps. I am grateful I did not have to face that test."

"We are *shaapit*," she reminded him, a bit sadly. "There is no fighting such a thing."

Raising his head to meet her eyes, he replied with some emphasis, "No; we are not *shaapit,* and in any event, I will fight it, if I damned well please."

"Damn-your-eyes," she teased. "No one can say that Englishmen are meek."

He smiled, slightly, and tucked her hand in his arm, as they continued their walk along the path—the gesture felt very intimate, for someone like her, but she did not withdraw her hand.

He offered, "You must think it is ironic, that my wife died of it, and yet I am running the opium trade, out of Canton. I can't blame you; I think it is ironic, too."

But she only shook her head, slowly. "No; even I understand there is a place for it—a good use. The Missionary's wife became ill with the wasting disease, and toward the end, she would take opium, to ease the pain. The Reverend hated the opium trade, and what it did to people, but he knew its value, in such a situation." She explained, "He believes the evil lies in the riches to be made, and how it makes the people listless, and less attentive to God."

"He sounds like a very wise man."

"You must not bring harm to him," she cautioned. "Please, James."

"I will do my best. The man sent me my wife, and I am grateful beyond measure."

"I haven't been a very good wife," she admitted.

"I know that you won't start taking opium, and that's enough for me."

She had to smile, at his stubbornness. "How can you know that I will bear you children? I had no children, with Abhay."

"It doesn't sound like he was home, much—which makes me wonder about his intelligence. And in any case, we can always adopt." After a slight pause, he added, "Sir Jost and his wife adopted a little girl."

"The Dutchman is a devil," she pronounced, in a grim tone. "You will not tell me of his supposed kindness, and try to change my mind on the subject."

He tilted his head. "I just thought I'd mention."

The shadows were beginning to lengthen, and yet, Kanika lingered with her companion, despite the fact that the plan to draw him downriver had been stymied. It hardly mattered—their goal had been obtained; if the Commander was lingering here with her, then he wasn't scouring the river, looking for Hahn, who was—by now—safely away to Ghazipur, and setting the factory ablaze.

Hard on this thought, the Commander bent his head to hers, and asked, "Can you tell me where your cohort is? I'm afraid it is important."

"I will not," she replied in an even tone.

"I am sorry for it," he said, and then took a step back, bringing his hands up, so as to adjust his hat.

She watched him, puzzled by the abrupt movement away from her, but then she was suddenly surrounded by four men, who'd emerged from the surrounding bushes to quickly seize her.

Furiously, she struggled against them—so furiously, that they were forced to take her to the ground, so as to subdue her.

As they held her down, so as to bind her hands, she could hear the Commander advise, "Careful; she carries a knife."

CHAPTER 30

She was furious, but Kanika has learned, long ago, to control her fury, because when one was operating under a strong set of emotions one made fatal errors—it was rather a failing of her people, unfortunately.

And so, she was silent, as she was bound and gagged, and roughly hauled to her feet. In the fading light, a man stepped forward, and indicated to the others that they were to take her aboard a nearby houseboat, that was tied to the makeshift dock. Kanika easily recognized the grey-eyed servant, who'd waited upon the Commander at the banquet—and who'd later walked with Millie.

Her stony gaze fixed on the distant horizon, Kanika gave no indication of her thoughts, as she was hauled along toward the boat. So; it seemed this unassuming man held power, even over the Commander. Despite her husband's betrayal, Kanika knew with complete certainty that the last thing he wanted was to have her roughly handled by a group of grim-faced men. He'd no choice, it seemed, and therefore this other man's power was greater than even that of the mighty British East India Company.

And so, Kanika thought, *much is now revealed; it seems the Commander fears what this unassuming man will do to me. But this unassuming man is dealing with a Kshatriya of Nair, and so, we shall see.*

"Take her aboard," the grey-eyed man said, in a terse tone, and then turned to the Commander. "Thank you. You will be hearing from me shortly."

"Instead, I would like to accompany you," the Commander replied steadily. "This involves me."

The other man said rather dismissively, "I think not; I am afraid the situation is urgent, and therefore, it will not be pleasant."

But still, the Commander did not move. "It had better be; this woman is my wife."

The other man was silent for a moment, staring at the Commander. "What nonsense is this?"

"It is not nonsense—this woman is my wife. I have the marriage lines, to prove it."

Now it was the other man who was furious, and he took a menacing step forward. "You are collaborating with the enemy; it is treason, sir. It cannot be clearer that she is Rochon's agent, in a massive operation. I am ashamed to say that you have been duped."

The Commander listened, unimpressed. "Whether or not this is true, the fact remains that she is my wife."

In a low voice, the other man threatened, "We are not going to lose England to Napoleon because you've been bewitched by a concubine, Commander."

"I would ask that you not take that tone with me, sir."

There was a long moment of tense silence, whilst neither man moved a muscle, and Kanika held her breath. The grey-eyed man finally ground out, "Very well. You may attend her interrogation, if you wish."

"I do so wish," said the Commander.

The bundled Kanika aboard the waiting houseboat —flat-bottomed, and nondescript—and then saw her seated in a chair, her hands still bound behind her. She lifted her chin, and stared at the corner of the cramped cabin, careful not to look at the Commander. After that first, horrified fear that he'd betrayed her, she'd quickly come to the conclusion that he was—instead—coming to her rescue, and at great risk to himself. She wasn't certain what he'd planned—apparently, his position and power were being thrown up as a shield, to protect her—but it seemed clear that her fate still hung in the balance.

The grey-eyed man stood before Kanika, whilst the other men—and the Commander—stood along the cabin's perimeter, watching them.

With an abrupt gesture, the grey-eyed man yanked down her gag. "Tell me your name, if you please."

"I will tell you nothing," Kanika replied, in an even tone. "Give me back my dagger."

"Are you married to this man?"

"Which one?" she asked.

But the grey-eyed man was in no mood, and leaned over in a menacing way, his hands resting on the arms of her chair. "I'm afraid this is serious business, and I am a very serious man."

The Commander shifted, slightly, and with a twist of his mouth, the grey-eyed man added, "If you please, ma'am."

"I am indeed married to him," Kanika admitted. "This is why I would like my dagger back." May as well do what she could; if she was going to be executed, she should at least try to spare him the same fate.

"Yes. In fact, I believe that you wounded Sir Jost Van der Haar. He advises me to be wary."

"The Dutchman is a devil," she pronounced. "It is not a surprise to me, that you are allied with him."

"Who are your allies? Does the Nizam work against the British?"

Ah; all is not lost—I can still set the sharks against each other, Kanika suddenly realized, and allowed her eyelids to drop, as though she was suddenly wary. "Most assuredly not."

"Forgive me if I don't believe you. How many of the Cohong conspire with the Nizam?"

In a non-answer, she advised, "I have never met any of the Cohong; indeed, I had never met my husband-to-be." She paused. "It is well, I think; he does not seem to be very dependable."

"Answer my question; how many of the Cohong conspire with the Nizam?"

"I will not answer your question, because I do not know the answer."

"Very well, I will ask a question you do know the answer to; who was your contact, in arranging this scheme?"

"The Dutchman," she confessed. "You must seize him, immediately."

The grey-eyed man flicked at glance over at the Commander, as if to remind him that he'd expected nothing less, and then persisted, "Where did the opium in your dowry originate from? Ghazipur? Is the Nizam siphoning-off a portion from the production, there?"

Kanika pressed her lips together, but her stony

silence hid her satisfaction; this man had drawn the conclusion intended by the Reverend—although they'd meant for the Commander to draw it, instead. And now, when they received the grim news that the factory had burned down, it would seem to the British that the Nizam was the one who did it, in a panic to cover-up his own misdeeds. Hahn, of course, will have planted false evidence to further this theory, and all production of opium would necessarily come to an abrupt halt, with the main factory in ruins, and the participants believing each was betrayed by the other, so that there could be no resumption of their unholy alliance. The final marker, in the Reverend's plan.

She carefully hid her satisfaction, as her attention was abruptly drawn back to her interrogator, who was not at all happy with her reticence, but was prevented from using any more forceful techniques by the still, silent presence of her husband.

His face inches from her own, the grey-eyed man ground out, "You will tell me, here and now, or it will be the worse for you."

"This is harassment," the Commander protested.

With an abrupt gesture, the grey-eyed man stood up, and faced him. "You are treading on thin ice, Commander. Do not think that I cannot have you removed from your position."

Undaunted, the Commander replied, "Do not think

that I cannot give the order that you be held, at Fort William."

The other man regarded him with open incredulity. "We need answers, sir, and quickly. If our allies conspire against us, it is a very grave situation. I do not speak lightly, when I tell you that it is treason, to impede my work, here."

But the Commander gave no ground, and instead replied, "Your work is suspect, then. I have been a witness to many of these events, and yet I note you do not seek answers from me, sir."

There was a small silence, as the other man stared at him. "Do I understand that you are withholding information?"

The Commander bowed his head. "I have theories, only. I am in the process of verifying them."

The other man reviewed him for a long moment. "Tell me of your theories, then."

"Very well. I do not think our allies, in this venture, are betraying us. I think, instead, that we are being set against each other by clever thieves."

With a dismissive gesture, the other man scoffed, "You have been duped, sir; this is an international scheme, with many working parts."

But the Commander stood firm, and only shook his head. "No. Instead, I think it is you, sir, who are being duped."

After a moment's thought, the other man crossed his arms. "Very well; I will give you five minutes."

In an even tone, the Commander explained, "My wife is a Nairian, from Kerala, and—regrettably—many of her kinfolk were killed in the ought-nine uprising, there. As a form of revenge, I believe she is working with a fellow Nairian to disrupt trading relations, between the Company and its trading partners."

The other man frowned. "And?"

The Commander spread his hands. "And that is the entirety of the scheme. They are bold thieves, who rely on deception, and misdirection."

With a frown, the other man contemplated him in silence for a moment. "Yet, it is indisputable that she was married to the old Nizam, and was then contracted to marry one of the Cohong. It is hard to imagine that this was mere coincidence."

Unmoving, the Commander replied, "But was she? The Hong was certainly persuaded that she was the Nizam's widow, and that she could provide him access to the fields of Patna. However, I have found that I cannot verify either of these things."

His brows drawn together in incredulity, the grey-eyed man prompted, "You don't think it is true?"

"I am not yet certain, whether it is true, or not true, but I am inclined to believe it is not."

To his credit, the other man studied the floor for a moment, thinking this over. "So—this may have been a house of cards, built on one tale atop the other."

"I believe so."

Slowly, the other man raised his head. "Yet—even if this were the case—I can still see Rochon's hand, in this. The scheme is very well thought-out, and required a great deal of staging."

"I am inclined to believe that Rochon hasn't the slightest notion of any of this."

With an impatient sound, the grey-eyed man allowed his skepticism to show. "So; we have two Nairians, out for revenge? That is the scheme? And they have managed to wreak such havoc?"

Please, don't mention the Reverend, thought Kanika, who sat, stone-faced, during this recital. *Please, don't mention the Reverend.*

"Yes," said the Commander. "As I said, I believe they are clever thieves."

"And yet you married her?"

Bowing his head, the Commander replied, "As a means of control, yes."

With a sardonic smile, the other pointed out, "It does not seem to be working very well."

"I would agree, and I take full responsibility."

The grey-eyed man turned his gaze to Kanika, where it rested thoughtfully. "I will admit that I find your theory unbelievable, Commander—especially in light of what has happened. But you are no fool, and it beggars belief, that you would allow your partiality for a woman to jeopardize world events. And so, let us bring the Nizam before us, and hear some answers."

"I am in full agreement," said the Commander.

The other man turned to face him again. "Please be advised, however, that your wife will suffer the consequences for her criminal acts, one way or the other. Either she allies with an enemy, and commits treason, or she is a thief, who has caused a great deal of destruction."

"A thief, merely," the Commander asserted. "And I would ask that her punishment be tempered by the fact she is my wife, and that she was largely unsuccessful, in her aim."

Twisting his mouth, the grey-eyed man retorted, "You have an interesting definition of success, sir. The Company's largest transport ship has been destroyed."

But the Commander did not falter. "I cannot see how you could pin such a thing on my wife, sir. She was under heavy guard, at all times, as the ship's Captain, himself, will attest."

The other man narrowed his eyes. "There is also the small matter of fifty chests of opium, destroyed."

But the Commander tilted his head, again. "I would be very surprised to discover that the bulk of the content was indeed opium, as opposed to a likely-looking substitute. These Nairians had no means of access, to such a large quantity of opium."

With an open show of skepticism, the other man asked, "And everyone was fooled, on all sides of the trade? You tell an incredible tale, Commander."

"Incredible, in its boldness," Kanika's husband agreed. "Indeed, it was the very reason that it worked."

CHAPTER 31

And so, Kanika had landed once again in Fort William, only this time, the grey-eyed man was taking no chances, and she was being detained in the brig—a fortified, block building, with iron bars on the windows. She'd gleaned that they were endeavoring to arrange for the Nizam's visit to the Fort for the following morning; time was of the essence, and —either way—it was imperative that the truth be discerned.

The grey-eyed man could not know, of course, that his precautions were unnecessary; Kanika had no plans to escape the Fort this time, for the simple reason that her dramatic arrest took all scrutiny away from Hahn. And Hahn was even now in the process of destroying the factory at Ghazipur, and planting false evidence that would implicate the Nizam. The timing was perfect, since the British were now known to be asking questions, and it would look as though the Nizam had panicked, and sought to destroy all evidence of his double-dealing.

Therefore, it seemed that—despite the fact the Commander had figured-out the Reverend's plan—it was all going to work out exactly as the Reverend had predicted. The grey-eyed man was already skeptical of the Commander's "ordinary thieves" theory, and this new evidence would—hopefully—sow immediate distrust amongst the trading partners, no matter what the Commander attempted to argue. The British alliance with the Nizam—and the Cohong, as well— would be damaged beyond repair, and the opium trade would come to an abrupt halt, whilst the factions fought with each other. *We've managed to set the sharks against each other, after all,* she thought. *It may not have gone exactly as we'd expected, but little in life does.*

And—as an added benefit—Hahn's false evidence would show that the Commander was wrong—even though, in truth, he'd guessed correctly. The others would look upon him as her dupe—unreliable, and easily misled—and therefore he'd be discredited, which was another marker, in the Reverend's plan. It was a shame, that he'd be disgraced, but—as the

Reverend himself had pointed out—it would be the best thing for him, to be extricated from his crucial role in this evil trade. He would have to resign, and they'd hopefully give his position to an incompetent second-son, instead. The Commander was a rare man, the Reverend had told them, and therein lay the problem.

He is a rare man, Kanika thought—*and I believe he sincerely loves me. But it seems unlikely that he will ever forgive me, once I he realizes that I have brought about his disgrace.*

Therefore, it was with mixed emotions that she rose to greet him, as he entered her cell, to visit her. *Stay strong,* she reminded herself, as his concerned gaze swept over her. *Much is at stake, and we are almost there.*

They sat down together, side-by-side on the cot. "Are you all right?" he asked gently. "I couldn't argue, when he insisted that you be detained, here."

"I am very well," she assured him. "I lived in a cave, once, when I was hiding from the Dutchman."

He offered-up a smile, that didn't quite meet his eyes. "Did you? The worst I can say is that I had to sleep on deck, when I was a midshipman."

She raised her brows. "That does not sound like a punishment, to me."

"I suppose it all depends on the weather." He reached into his waistcoat, to pull out a tied-up handkerchief from within it, and then began to unfold the square of linen. "I have brought you a fig."

He handed it over, and she cradled it in her lap—and then found that she had to bow her head for a moment, because her mouth was trembling.

Concerned, he placed his warm hand over hers. "Are you angry?" he asked.

She took a long breath, so as to compose herself. "No—I am not angry. You did what you felt you must, and I can see—I can see that you are trying to shield me." She didn't mention, of course, that the main reason she could hold no grudges was because she was soon to prevail, in this chess match, and that he would soon suffer a miserable defeat.

"It is a damnable situation," he said quietly. "And I am sorrier than I can say."

She looked up at him. "Who was that man? No one spoke his name."

It seemed to her that he chose his words carefully, when providing an answer. "He has a great deal of influence, unfortunately. I am asked to report to him, about the things I observe, and to answer his questions."

She knit her brow. "He is a soldier?"

"No; he works directly for the British King."

"And you don't like him, much."

"No. But I don't envy him his job."

Reminded, she fumed, "He has my *katar*." This annoyed her more than she could say; she'd had it with her, ever since her coming-of-age ceremony.

"I took it, back," he assured her. "And it will be returned to you—I give you my word."

Her eyes searched his. "But no time soon, I think. Especially if I am to go to prison."

It seemed that he had been waiting for her to broach this subject, because he said with quiet intensity, "I think it would be best if you tell him the truth, Kanika. Your plan can no longer work, if all parties now know that it is all an elaborate sham. I think it would be best if you confess the scheme, and plead for mercy."

She admitted, "Hahn knew that you knew, when I told him your story about the sharks, at sea. I thought it was only a coincidence—that you told such a tale— but he was worried."

He shrugged, slightly. "I'd guessed."

"You are the better chess player," she acknowledged.

He tightened his hand on hers, where they rested in her lap. "I will defend you, as best I can, but I imagine it won't be long before suspicion is cast your way, with respect to the old Nizam's death. In fact, I'm rather surprised the subject has not yet arisen."

Hearing this, she raised her brows. "We did not kill the Nizam, James."

"He died in the fire, Kanika. It does not look well."

She shook her head. "No—the Nizam was old, and he died when it was his time—it was what set the plan into action. The Reverend had sources that told him the old Nizam was gravely ill, and so all was held in readiness, for when he died." She met his eyes sincerely. "The Reverend was very careful to avoid causing any deaths—it would be a grave sin."

But he was frowning at her, in disbelief. "What of setting a bomb aboard the ship, then?"

"Everyone was on deck at the time, and so, the sleeping quarters were empty. We were very careful, that no one was killed."

He lifted his hand to run it over his face, and she felt a pang—he was tired, and worried, and his worries were soon to be multiplied, many times over. *Stay strong—it is for the best*, she fiercely reminded herself.

"Be that as it may, it will be very hard to convince the— the gentleman from the King, that you were not somehow involved in the Nizam's death. And the man is no fool, Kanika; I can insist you are merely a thief, but he will note that you've never attempted to steal anything, and will therefore conclude that your motives are more nefarious."

She ventured, "You can't tell him the truth? That we

sought only to disrupt the opium trade, and not to enrich ourselves?"

"No. Your punishment would be much more severe, believe me. They'd dare not treat you lightly, for fear of inspiring other such attempts." He lifted his hand, and drew her head against his, temple to temple. "Not to mention I will look the fool, for having married you."

She nodded, and wished—oh, how she wished—that they were two ordinary people, and there was not the fate of a country—two countries—to consider. Truly, it seemed that there was no easy path forward, for them. It was *shaapit*, and there was nothing to be done.

His next words seemed to echo her thoughts. "I will argue that you should be held under house arrest, under my auspices, but it seems unlikely that he will agree."

She nodded, unable to find her voice, because—by this time tomorrow—no one would be listening to him, or inclined to grant him any favors at all. Therefore, with all sincerity, she whispered, "I am sorry, to have brought such shame upon you."

His head still pressed against hers, he replied, "I wouldn't have changed a single moment, Kanika. It's the truth."

"I, too," she said, steadily, even as she knew he

would swiftly change his mind, once he learned of the factory's destruction. *I was a warrior, once,* she thought; *single-minded, and furious. But now I see that nothing is quite so simple—it was rather foolish, to think that it was.*

"Until tomorrow, then." He gathered her up into an embrace, as they sat on the cot, and she'd a sense of poignancy, as though he was well-aware that tomorrow loomed very ominously. She lay her head against his shoulder, closing her eyes as she breathed in his scent, and couldn't help saying, "I wish—I wish tomorrow would never come."

He withdrew, to smile at her in a reassuring fashion —even as she saw that again, the smile didn't quite reach his eyes. "We'll come about; please try not to worry. You are my wife, and the King's man has need of my cooperation, in this part of the world. He is not in England, and so that is a benefit, for us."

She nodded, unable to speak, and then he placed a quick hand against her cheek, before he rose to ask the guard to open the door, turning one last time to glance at her, before the door clanged shut behind him.

Kanika sat in the dim stillness for a moment, and then lay down on the meager cot, fighting the unfamiliar prickling of tears, as she re-lived what they'd said to each other. The Reverend had warned them there would be setbacks, and that they must remain steadfast, but here was a completely unexpected setback—the worst one of all—that she would fall in love with the man whose life she intended to ruin. It was indeed *shaapit*—but she mustn't think of the old ways; she must remember what the Reverend had said, about how the Commander's ruin would be the best thing that could possibly happen to him, so as to save his soul. She must remember this, and remain strong—the Reverend had taught her that love endures all things, and that it was a blessing, to be tested. It was only—it was only so unfortunate, that she was to be tested so thoroughly; that she'd been fated to meet the Commander at this time, and in this place.

Enough, she thought, and turned over abruptly, to face the wall; *tomorrow will be difficult enough, without making it worse, with foolish regrets.*

Hard on this thought, she closed her eyes and focused on sleep, only to be startled by the sound of a key in the lock.

"Many thanks," a man's voice said, and Kanika suddenly sat bolt upright in the bed, scarcely believing her ears, as she stared at the figure that filled the doorway.

"*You*," she breathed in astonishment.

"Me," agreed Sir Jost van der Haar, as he regarded her with a cynical smile. "You are to come with me—I take you away, from here."

Scrambling out of bed, she backed against the opposite wall, as far away from him as possible. "I—I don't believe you—what are you doing here?"

The Dutchman bowed his head in ironic acknowledgment. "The British Commander, he has asked me to honor my *niyama*."

Kanika stared at the Dutchman, unable to come up with a response, for a moment. In all honesty, this was an unlooked-for boon —the news of the factory's destruction would mean that the full fury of the grey-eyed man would fall upon her; not only would the Commander be disgraced, but she would be locked away in prison, and with no further ado. She and Hahn would plan for an escape, of course, but it would take some careful planning, since the British would be well-aware she was adept at slipping away from them. How much easier, if she were to simply disappear before the messenger arrived with the bad news, on the morrow.

Slowly, she lowered her arms from the wall, and frowned, slightly. "How will you manage it?"

"Me, I go where I wish," the Dutchman explained,

and then jerked his head. "Come, come. We must make haste."

And, it seemed that he did go where he wished, because the sentry at cell door made no protest, as Kanika followed the Dutchman out, and then through the assembly-yard, her companion walking along as though he hadn't a care in the world.

Stepping softly, she hurried after him, warily watching for any movement from the shadows, until they came to the gate, where a wooden-faced solider nodded, and then opened it just enough to allow them to slip through. "Cap'n."

"Many thanks," said Sir Jost quietly.

They began to head across the maidan toward the river, and when she felt it was safe to speak, Kanika whispered, "Where do we go?"

Her companion replied, "My ship, she is anchored off the Bay. I am to take you anywhere you wish to go."

So; it seemed the Commander had decided to spare her the repercussions that he saw coming, and had instead arranged for her escape—even as it meant that he would appear foolish, for having trusted her. *I had the sense he was saddened,* she thought; *and now I know it was because he wasn't certain he would ever see me again.*

And, of course, such a thing was entirely possible; after tomorrow, she'd no reason to look for him, nor he for her. Even as it engendered a painful twist, within her breast, she reminded herself that it was the best possible ending, out of all the poor choices which were available. They were *shaapit,* and she'd been foolish to fall in love with him, and to long for some way that they could live their lives together.

Sir Jost interrupted her thoughts. "He gave me your dagger, to return to you, but I do not wish to give it to you yet." He glanced over at her. "My arm, it has the scar."

"I'm sorry I stabbed you," she offered. "I was angry, and I wasn't a Christian, yet."

"Still, I will hold your dagger, until you go."

"You need not fear; I am grateful that you do this. You have every reason to refuse to help me."

"I made the promise, to Abhay," he replied, as though it was the only explanation necessary.

She walked a few steps, and then ventured, "What happened, between you? Abhay never told me."

For a moment, she thought he wouldn't answer, but then he said, "I met a man who changed me—changed how my mind thought. Me, I was ready to change, but Abhay, he was not ready to change."

A bit sadly, she agreed, "No, Abhay was not someone who could change." As they approached the docks, she offered, "I, too, met a man who changed me. He was a holy man, and he took the dagger from my hand, and spoke of forgiveness." Slowly, she shook her head. "It was very difficult, to think in this way, after all the terrible things that have happened. But I must try, I think."

The Dutchman cocked his head. "*Ja*; we are alive, and Abhay is not."

"Yes—there is that." She glanced up, again. "I hear that you took Aditi to England, and found her a husband."

"This is the truth."

"It is indeed a miracle," she marveled.

"Assuredly," he agreed, with a small, smile.

"And—and you are wed, too." She strained to remember. "You have a daughter?"

He nodded, and then said abruptly, "She was Abhay's daughter, but now she is mine."

She stared at him in astonishment. "Oh—I did not know. He never mentioned her."

He gave her a look, to suggest that this should not be a surprise, considering Kanika had been his wife, but the Dutchman was not to know that such a thing would not be shocking, amongst her people. And so instead, she said, "You are a good man, to honor your *niyama*."

"I am married to the finest woman."

With some consternation, she admitted, "I wish I was the finest woman."

"The British Commander, he thinks you are." This,

said with palpable doubt. "Although he said you will be angry, and that I must not allow you to do something foolish." He nodded, in self-satisfaction. "And so, I do not give you your dagger."

"I am not angry," she protested. "Instead, I am grateful to you."

"Me, I do not think you will be grateful," he replied, and then lifted the canvas flap on his tender-boat, so that she could board.

Readily, she ducked her head under the canvas, and clambered aboard, only to be brought up short. At the boat's stern sat Hahn, his attitude one of dejection, and an iron manacle, locked around his ankle.

"*Hahn*," she breathed in acute dismay, "What has happened?"

"The Dutchman was waiting for me at the factory," Hahn confessed. "The Commander knew I was coming."

CHAPTER 33

*U*nable to help it, Kanika came forward, to sink down at Hahn's feet—so acutely disappointed that she couldn't find words, for a moment. "Oh—oh, Hahn; I am so sorry. I should have listened to you—you were right, to be wary."

He lowered his voice. "You didn't tell the Commander of the plan, Neeka?"

"No—of course not. But he is very shrewd, Hahn. He can see ten moves ahead, and he must have guessed—no one knows better than he, that the factory at Ghazipur is the key."

Hahn's eyes slid toward Sir Jost, who leaned against the gunwale, watching them. "He has orders that I be chained, while we are transported."

"We will set sail," the Dutchman offered in a genial tone. "And you will forget these problems, yes?"

Kanika calculated the chances of outwitting Sir Jost —and sparing Hahn from drowning, in the process— and decided that it would be a better strategy to try to enlist the Dutchman, instead; after all, they'd had a surprisingly civil conversation, on the way over here.

She shifted, so that she could address the other man. "You used to run opium—for someone named Rochon."

The Dutchman's gaze rested on her thoughtfully, even as he made no comment.

"You stopped, because the trade is evil. It is evil—it causes famines, and the opium makes the people listless. Hahn and I, we are trying to put a stop to it—to set the sharks against each other."

Sir Jost cocked his head. "Me, I do not know what this means."

Encouraged by his willingness to listen, Kanika continued, "It means we are trying to make the British and the Nizam and the Cohong quarrel with each other —sow distrust, so that they will stop this trade."

The Dutchman nodded thoughtfully. "It is a good plan. You are not strong enough to stop them, and so you make them stop each other."

This seemed a hopeful sign—and, after all, no one would know better how to sow mistrust and chaos than a pirate—and so Kanika ventured, "Could you help us? We can still set the sharks; we can burn down the Company's Records House, here in Calcutta, and make it appear that it was the Nizam who did it—destroyed it, so as to hide his double-dealing. It would take only a few hours."

Eagerly, Hahn added, "And then we will board your ship, and not give you a moment's trouble."

But Sir Jost shook his head, slightly. "No. The British, they will think the Commander arranged for this."

"That is not a problem," Hahn explained. "We seek to have him discredited, and removed from his position."

But Kanika had paused with this thought, and was contemplating the floorboards with a knit brow. "He is right, Hahn. They will suspect the Commander arranged for my escape—too many people have seen Sir Jost, at the Fort. That man—the King's man—will hold the Commander responsible, if we destroy the Records House. He will have him arrested."

There was a small pause. "Who is the King's man?" Hahn asked, in no little confusion.

"Oh—there is a man here, who works for the English King, and the Commander is very wary of him, and of his power. This man thinks we work for Rochon, who is his enemy, in their war." She paused. "I think the Commander feared what the King's man would do to me, to make me confess the plan, and that is why he married me. And then—when the King's man arrested me—the Commander tried to convince him we were only thieves, and not working for his enemy." Frowning, she added, "The Dutchman is right; it will not look well for the Commander, if we burn down the Records House."

"And we would not wish this?" asked Hahn, who still seemed rather confused.

Slowly, Kanika shook her head. "I can't let that happen—he would go to prison. I can't betray him, in such a way." She glanced up at him. "Forgive me, Hahn."

Loyally, Hahn declared, "There is nothing to forgive, Neeka—we need only make a new plan."

Sir Jost raised his brows at this. "This new plan; it must include sailing away with me, yes?"

"Perhaps not," Kanika ventured. "Just because we didn't manage to burn the Factory—or the Records House—it doesn't mean we can't still turn them against each other. Much of the plan was a success, after all; the Hong was willing to marry me in secret—"

"You were to marry a Cohong?" asked Sir Jost in surprise.

"Yes," she replied, rather impatiently. "Hahn posed as an envoy from the Nizam, and arranged for it. Hahn told the Hong that the Nizam was going to smuggle opium, without the British knowing, and the Hong agreed."

"*Verdomme,*" said Sir Jost, in all admiration. "This was a good plan."

"It was a very good plan, until we underestimated the Commander," Hahn added. "He worked-out what we'd intended, before we could finish it."

"Yet, we have succeeded, for much of it," Kanika insisted. "And so, it could still work; I can demand to be present, when the Nizam comes to meet with the British. I will be furious—I am the blighted bride; I was promised riches, but instead the Hong abandoned me, and I am left with nothing. I will tell the British that the Nizam agreed to the Hong's plan, and then I will show them your false evidence—"

"Sir Jost took the false evidence," Hahn reluctantly informed her.

Kanika's gaze flew to meet the Dutchman's. "Please —you must let us do this; there is still a chance that we can disrupt the trade, without the Commander going to prison."

But Sir Jost cocked his head, and said, almost apologetically, "I do not think this is a good plan. Me, I have no wish to cause such problems for the East India Company." He paused, "Or for the Commander."

Knowing that the comment was directed towards her, Kanika said in all seriousness, "He is their key man, but he does not like the trade, either. He thinks the money is needed for this war—the one in Europe. He is very stubborn about it."

But the big man only crossed his arms. "I say that this is not a good plan, and you must think of a better one."

Kanika was going to protest, but Hahn—ever adept at reading people—held up a hand, to stay her. "Tell me, Dutchman," he asked, in all politeness. "Do you have a better plan?"

"Assuredly," the other man replied.

As Kanika blinked in surprise, Sir Jost continued, "I have sailed to many places, and I have seen many things." His intent gaze rested upon them, a trace of amusement, lurking therein. "I hear many things, but I keep them to myself, because I may have need of them, someday." He tilted his head. "There are many secrets, in such a country, and with such riches to be made."

Kanika stared at him. "What is it that you know?"

"The new Nizam, he controls the fields of Padua. But he has no heir, as yet—no sons of age. It would create the situation of chaos, if he is taken down, by an enemy. The British cannot allow this."

Frowning, Kanika asked in confusion, "But—why would the Nizam be taken down by an enemy?"

With a small smile, Sir Jost explained, "Because of the diamonds."

CHAPTER 34

And so, once again, Kanika found herself hiding in the spreading branches of a banyan tree, and watching the road below.

Her original thought was to dress in finery, and imperiously demand entrance to the Fort for the Nizam's visit, but Hahn was worried that the Commander—since he was wise to their ways—would thwart this intent, and prevent her from being anywhere in the vicinity of the Nizam—not to mention that the grey-eyed man would no doubt throw her back into the brig, the moment he laid eyes on her. Therefore, since the Nizam would travel to the Fort by elephant, an alternate plan was hatched, and Kanika had climbed the tree in the dark hours of the early morning, so as to find a likely branch, and settle-in to wait.

As the day began to dawn, she had plenty of time to consider the Commander's reaction, when he discovered that they'd managed to talk Sir Jost out of his task—or at least delay it, for a day. But—thinking about this—she decided that he wouldn't be angry, because they were incapable of being angry with each other, as events had already shown. After all, she thought he'd be angry, after discovering that they'd destroyed the factory, and that he'd never wish to speak with her, again. She'd been wrong, though; even though he'd known that she'd planned his disgrace, he wasn't angry—instead, he was worried that she would be the one who was angry, when she discovered that he'd thwarted the plan, and had managed to checkmate her. He was worried that she'd never wish to speak with him, ever again.

But he was also wrong, she thought; *I am not angry—I never could be, it would be like being angry with myself. We love each other, despite everything, and love always trusts, always perseveres—that's what the Reverend said. Although I think it was St. Paul, who said it, which reminds me that if nothing else, at least we have St. Paul, in common.*

But the Commander hadn't been so certain of love's power, last night, and that was why he'd seemed so saddened, to her. He'd promised that they would work it out, and be together—he'd given her his oath on it, as a matter of fact—but he'd known that the one thing he could not do, was to compel her to do something she didn't wish to. He would never force her to stay married to him.

Foolish man, she thought, smiling to herself; *to think so little of me, and of my own oath, given to him in that dark church, on that night of nights. He can be forgiven, though; he has no understanding of what an oath means to a Kshatriya of Nair, after all.*

The road below her gradually began to become busier, and she stretched her length along the branch, so as to not be so easily visible. At long last, the Nizam's procession came into view—an elephant, dressed elaborately in cloth-of-gold, and surrounded by outriders and guards, with the Nizam riding atop it in a howdah, dressed in splendid finery. He'd not be happy, about being summoned to the British Fort like a naughty child, and would want to impress upon his trading partners that he was a powerful ruler, and not to be treated with such disrespect.

Carefully timing her actions, Kanika drew her *katar*, and then waited until the howdah was directly beneath her. As lightly as she could, she then dropped down onto the platform, landing atop the Nizam with some force. Immediately, she snaked an arm around the startled man's neck, and pressed her *katar* to his throat. "Stay still," she warned.

The elephant continued on, unfazed, but the

outrider behind, who'd seen her actions, shouted an alarm, as he drew his sword.

Whilst the Nizam sat, frozen with fear, she told him quickly, "Do not be alarmed; I will not hurt you. Instead, I must give you warning, about the smuggling of the Golconda diamonds."

Her words did not seem to reassure him much, as his fear turned instead into an wary and alarmed dismay. "Who are you?"

She lessened the *katar*'s pressure on his throat, and replied, "I am a concubine, from the court of the Rajah of Sattara. "I seek to warn you—and the British—that the Rajah knows of your betrayal, and prepares for war."

Carefully, she withdrew the blade, and noted with satisfaction that he'd stilled, acutely dismayed, and seemed to be considering her words with no little consternation. "I am sorry to startle you, but I could think of no other way to catch your attention, and to gain entry. I must be careful; the Rajah's men pursue me. The diamonds—"

"Say no more," the Nizam said hurriedly, and glanced around to ensure she'd not been overheard. "Come with me, then, and you may give your message to the British."

The outriders stood around them with their swords drawn—although they couldn't easily reach her, atop the elephant, which was why the strategy had been chosen.

"It is naught," the Nizam called out to them, in a reassuring tone; "I know this woman—she is a bold concubine, is all."

His men lowered their swords and exchanged amused glances, and then the elephant was prodded forward, once again.

And so, when the stately procession entered the gates of Fort William, where the Company's ranking personnel were ceremoniously assembled to receive the Nizam of Bengal, they were very much surprised to behold Kanika, seated behind the Nizam, her manner calm and composed.

The Commander stood alongside the Governor-General in the assembly yard, and he immediately met her eyes, his impassive expression not betraying the fact that he was not so much surprised, as he was heartily amused—she could sense it, even at this distance. In turn, Kanika had to fight to maintain her own expression, and suppress a smile. *Finally, finally, I have outwitted him,* she thought; *we will laugh about it, together—that is, if this day does not end in ruin, for the both of us.*

CHAPTER 35

"Your Excellency." The very correct Governor-General stepped forward, to greet the Nizam with a small bow. "How very good it is to see you again."

"We must speak privately," the Nizam replied, in a blunt tone, and then remembered to add belatedly, "Governor."

"Wouldn't you care to dine, first?" the ranking British representative asked, with polite surprise.

"No—it cannot wait."

The Nizam clapped, and one of his personal guards brought forth a ladder, to assist him down from the elephant, with Kanika following along after him. No one seemed to notice that this particular personal guard was a newcomer—a wiry man, who flashed an insolent grin at the Nizam's favored concubine.

"Please; this way, then," the Governor-General offered, with a respectful gesture. "We can hold our business, and then have refreshments in my private dining room."

The Nizam nodded, distracted, as he gathered his robes over his arms. "The girl comes, too."

The Governor-General raised his heavy white brows, at such a breach of protocol, but bowed to Kanika with all politeness. "Ma'am."

They were escorted into the Government House, and then upstairs to the elegantly appointed dining room, where Kanika was not at all surprised to discover that the grey-eyed man awaited them, standing by the windows, and discreetly dressed in an ordinary suit of clothes.

Immediately upon sighting Kanika, he did an admirable job of hiding his extreme surprise, before immediately gesturing to an aide, "This woman belongs in the brig. Return her there, please."

"She stays," the Nizam insisted, and then added, with a sharp look, "She brings information."

"I have no doubt, she does," the other man observed a bit sourly, and then turned his rather pointed attention to the Commander, who'd entered the room behind them. "Is this your doing, sir?"

"It is not, sir," the Commander replied.

The grey-eyed man held the other's gaze for a long

moment, in an indication that he wasn't certain he believed the answer. "How did she escape from the brig, Commander?"

At sea, the Governor-General drew down his brows. "*This* woman escaped from the brig? *Our* brig?"

"It is not very secure," Kanika informed the older man, with a show of disapproval.

But the Nizam was listening to this exchange with narrowed eyes. "Was it the Rajah of Sattara, who commanded that she be imprisoned?"

The Governor's brows snapped up. "What's this? The Rajah of Sattara?"

"Take her away," the grey-eyed man interrupted impatiently, and then turned to the Nizam. "She fills your ears with lies, Excellency, in order to save her own skin."

"She stays," the Nizam insisted in a grim tone. "I do not know who lies, but I intend to find out."

Rather aghast, the Governor-General intervened, "Please, gentleman—let us be seated; no need to throw about accusations."

"I am afraid I cannot oblige you, Governor," the grey-eyed man said, in a deceptively polite voice. "I have requested that the Nizam be called before us, precisely for the purpose of throwing about accusations."

"*You* accuse *me*? The Nizam countered in outrage,

and took a menacing step toward the other. "I will not stand for this—you have no reason—"

But the grey-eyed man only countered, "Then you will explain, please, why you allied this woman to one of the Cohong, and then arranged for fifty chests of opium, as her dowry."

The Nizam stilled, and stared at the other in amazement. His gaze then skewed to Kanika, for a brief moment. "*This* woman?"

"Do not feign ignorance, please. You brought her here with you today, after all."

The other man continued to stare at him, in angry disbelief. "You know not of what you speak. This woman is a concubine, from the court of the Rajah of Sattara. She brings important information."

But the grey-eyed man wasn't having it, and retorted in a sharp tone, "Do not play me for a fool, Excellency; she is your aunt by marriage—she was your uncle's fourth wife."

Outraged, the Nizam declared, "You *lie*—"

Hoping to soothe the escalating situation, the Governor-General spread his hands. "A mere misunderstanding, perhaps; when a man has many wives, it is possible to lose track—"

But the grey-eyed man said in a clipped tone, "No, it was not a mere misunderstanding, I am afraid. The Nizam, here, arranged for this woman to travel along the river routes, to avoid British scrutiny at the Port of Calcutta, and the Port of Canton. He sought to undermine our contracts."

"These are cursed lies," the Nizam pronounced, his voice rising. "And you will suffer, for them."

The sharks, tearing into each other, Kanika thought, and dared not meet Hahn's eye.

With an angry gesture, the Nizam indicated Kanika, with a jerk of his head. "Tell him," he directed her.

"Before everyone?" she ventured. "Is that wise?"

"Tell him," he repeated, in an implacable tone.

Choosing her words carefully, she said, "The Rajah of Sattara is very disappointed, in how the yields from his Golconda diamond mines have fallen off."

There was a sudden, strained silence, and Kanika carefully hid her satisfaction, behind a grave expression. Sir Jost—who heard every whisper—had learned of a clandestine operation, whereby a portion of the Rajah's diamonds were being siphoned-off from the mines he controlled in the Deccan Plateau. Siphoned-off by operatives employed by the British—as well as the Nizam—who had agreed to the scheme so as to lessen the Rajah's power, even as they increased their own. Needless to say, the Rajah would be most unhappy, to discover that he'd been duped by such a scheme, and an immediate war would be the certain result.

"What the *devil* do the Rajah's diamond mines have to do with anything?" asked the Governor-General, with understandable confusion.

Ignoring him, the grey-eyed man asked Kanika sharply, "How do you know of this?"

With a show of modesty, Kanika replied, "The Rajah seeks a Kshatriyan wife—it would add much to his prestige."

"You are bluffing," the grey-eyed man declared, and then indicated the Commander with a jerk of his chin. "You cannot marry the Rajah, if you are married to this man."

Astonished, the Governor-General turned to the Commander. "You are *married* to her?"

"I am," said the Commander, who'd said nothing, thus far.

A rare man, Kanika thought; *to be content only to listen, and discern, whilst the others are battling.*

"My congratulations, sir," the Governor-General offered formally. He then added politely, "A very lovely girl."

"Thank you," said the Commander.

But the grey-eyed man interrupted these niceties by offering, in a more conciliatory manner, "We have much to discuss, it seems, and I must apologize, Your Excellency, if I have been misled. It would be best, I think, to withdraw for a private conversation about these matters."

But things were to take an unexpected turn, as the Governor-General spoke with a more forceful tone, than he'd previously used. "See here; these are pressing matters, and it appears that I have been kept uninformed."

"There have been many, many lies," the Nizam agreed, his eyes narrowed, as they rested upon the grey-eyed man.

"I look to serve the King's business," the other man reminded the Governor-General. "And much of that business cannot be bruited about. My apologies, Governor, but oftentimes these matters call for discretion."

But the Governor-General was the ranking representative for the East India Company, and therefore was not intimidated by any references to a mere King. "Well, sir; speaking on behalf of the Company, I cannot be pleased that I have no knowledge of these subjects—which have obviously created division, amongst our trading partners. I will also say that I must heartily disapprove of any schemes that would interfere with the power structure, in this country. If you pit the Rajah against the other native rulers, such a course could only undermine the Company's interests."

Another shark joins in, Kanika thought with surprise; *and this one rather unexpected.*

"The Company's interests are not my interests," the grey-eyed man pronounced, without hesitation. "My interests lie with the King, and I will ask that you not interfere with my charter, sir."

But the Governor-General only rocked back on his heels. "It is hard to imagine, sirrah, that the King's interests and the Company's interests are so disparate. I insist that I be told what is going forward, here."

"My own interests lie with the diamonds," Kanika offered, a bit wistfully. "Perhaps the Rajah will give me one, for my service to him."

"Young lady, you mustn't accept jewelry from a man other than your husband," the Governor-General chided gently. "It is simply not done."

Surprised, Kanika regarded him with raised brows. "This is so? But surely, if I perform such a valuable service for the Rajah, I should be rewarded for it."

"What service is this?" the older man asked in confusion, and then could be seen to decide that perhaps it was best not to delve into this topic, with the lady's husband present. Instead, he turned to the others. "Gentlemen, perhaps it would be optimal if the three of us adjourned, to discuss these matters in privacy."

"Very well," said Kanika. "As for me, I will send a

message to the Rajah, along with my sincere apologies, for the strife that I have caused."

"Very proper, and right," the Governor-General said with approval, even as the Nizam and the grey-eyed man glanced at each other, in discreet alarm.

There was a small, tense silence, and no one moved. "Tell me your terms," the grey-eyed man said to Kanika, in a curt tone.

Immediately, Kanika's voice hardened. "My terms are these: a portion of the fields in Bengal will be dedicated to crops other than opium. The British will see to it that the farmers are paid the same price as they were paid for the opium."

The grey-eyed man nodded, as though relieved she sought nothing more. "This is a reasonable request, certainly. I can arrange matters so that one-fourth of the current fields will be dedicated to such use."

Behind him, Kanika saw the Commander tilt his head, very slightly.

"One-half," she demanded, her eyes narrowed.

With a show of exasperation, the grey-eyed man chided, "Young woman, I have a war to fight."

"And I have a people to feed."

"One-third, then, as a compromise," the Governor-General broke in. "If the Rajah is concerned about the breadth of the opium trade, he should be mollified; an uprising must be avoided, at all costs—it would be terrible for business."

In a significant manner, the Nizam addressed the grey-eyed man. "An uprising would be the least of it; if the Rajah were to hear of this, he would slit my throat, and seize the fields of Padua."

"Oh?" said the Governor-General, rather surprised. "Is the man that hot-at-hand?"

"He is much soothed, by his diamonds," Kanika offered.

The older man smiled, rather indulgently. "I suppose, my dear, that you can be forgiven for thinking about the man's diamonds, above all else."

Kanika returned his smile. "And if these terms are not honored by the British, I promise that the Rajah will be thinking about them above all else, also."

"No need to fear," the grey-eyed man assured her, in a heavy tone. "I give you my word, it will be done."

CHAPTER 36

One week later, Kanika found herself at a wedding reception—her own—which, ironically, was being held at the Government House in Fort William. The Governor-General had insisted that the Commander's wedding be celebrated in form, even as the Company's ranking officer wasn't quite certain how it had come about, in the first place.

They have their rituals, the English, thought Kanika, indulgently. *And who would have thought the Governor-General of the East India Company would become an ally, in the plan? The Reverend will be very much amused.*

She stood next to her husband in the receiving line —so handsome, in his formal clothes—and greeted each of the guests, who managed, for the most part, to hide their discreet astonishment behind polite masks.

An exception, of course, was found in the

Lieutenant-Colonel's wife, who immediately chided Kanika with all good humor, "You sly thing—carried off the palm, and with me all unaware."

"It was a secret," Kanika smiled. "I am sorry, that I could not say."

"Well, it's all very romantic," the woman pronounced, and then glanced rather doubtfully at the Commander. "Wouldn't think he had it in him."

"He is a very surprising man," Kanika agreed.

"I suppose he's set for life, now—I hear rumor that you're related to the Rajah of Sattara; I can only imagine the dowry, you must bring."

The woman paused with some significance, clearly hoping that Kanika would provide specifics, but Kanika only chided gently, "You mustn't believe everything you hear, ma'am."

Plying her fan, the older woman laughed aloud. "Now, where would be the fun in that?"

As Kanika smiled in response, the other took her hand. "My very best wishes," she declared warmly, and then did not hesitate to move on to the Commander, and lift her face, so that he was prompted to kiss her cheek.

They were coming to the last of the guests, and the Commander leaned in to ask, "How are you holding up?"

"Very well," Kanika replied easily, and did not

mention that she'd met more strangers in the past hour than the whole of her life, thus far. "And you?"

"I will confess that I do not enjoy this type of thing."

"Then you must take heart; you need suffer through no others."

"They will throw a farewell reception," he noted, in an unenthusiastic tone.

"Only one more, then," she amended.

They had decided, together, that he would resign his position, and instead seek to work in the Naval Office, in London. It was a compromise; he would use his talents to help his country's war effort in a more honorable way, and she would abide with him in London.

Their receiving line duties finished, Kanika's husband took her hand, and drew her over toward the windows, where they could avoid their guests for a few moments, and speak in private. "I have already sent an inquiry to the Naval Office—discreetly, of course; I would ask that you say nothing about our plans, as yet. And I have asked some of my contacts at the Colonial Club in London to give me the names of prominent members of the Indian community. We will make contact, once we are settled."

"Thank you—that is very thoughtful," said Kanika, and smiled to herself, because it seemed clear that the

British in London thought of India as one large country, when—in truth—it was many smaller countries. No matter; it seemed that her new husband was more determined to smooth her way than she was, and it was rather sweet—even as it seemed a bit foolish. After all, he was the one who'd observed that she was fearless.

"Is there food to be served, here? I was told there would be food."

With a smile, Kanika turned to behold Hahn, his expression polite, but his eyes gleaming with humor. He was dressed very correctly, in a British suit-of-clothes, and Kanika didn't dare ask where he'd stolen it.

"Hello," said Kanika graciously. "I don't believe I caught your name."

"I am but a poor fisherman," he replied, as he formally bowed over her hand, in the British fashion. "But I am thinking of becoming a pirate." Hahn had been mightily impressed with Sir Jost, mainly because the Dutchman had managed to capture him.

"Sir," said the Commander, who offered his hand. "Our home is always open to you."

"I won't come in the window," Hahn promised.

"Much appreciated. When do you return to Kerala?"

"Tomorrow. I will sail with the Dutchman, when he heads for home."

The Commander nodded in approval. "You bear no grudges, I see. I am glad."

Hahn shrugged his shoulders, slightly. "I can't afford to bear grudges, or I will wind up like Abhay." He then addressed Kanika, in their own language. "What shall I tell the Reverend, Neeka?"

"Tell him everything," she replied. "I think he will greatly enjoy the tale. And I will write to him, of course—I will tell him of England." Reminded, she urged, "You must write to me, also, Hahn—promise that you will." Unfortunately, this seemed unlikely—Hahn was Hahn, and would soon be caught up in his next adventure; hopefully he was only joking, about becoming a pirate.

"I will come visit England," he declared. "The women are pretty, and no one cares about castes."

"They do," she cautioned; "it is only not as obvious."

But they were suddenly interrupted, by an all-too-familiar voice, "Well; this is all very touching—although I confess it makes me uneasy, that I cannot discern what the two of you say to one another."

Startled, Kanika turned to behold the grey-eyed man, watching them with a faintly sardonic expression, as he stood at a small distance. She'd rather hoped that she need never see him again—he'd disappeared, after the contentious meeting with the Nizam, and even the Commander wasn't certain where he'd gone.

"Sir," said the Commander in a formal tone, as he stepped forward, to politely shake the other man's hand. "I trust you are well."

The other man's mouth twisted, slightly. "As well as I can be, I suppose. I have come to make an attempt to salvage the situation, so that it does not stand as an unmitigated loss, on my record."

"The situation appears to be well-in-hand, sir," the Commander disagreed, in a level tone. "I see no need to go over old ground."

The grey eyes glinted with humor. "No need to get your back up, Commander; I have come to make you an offer."

With some uneasiness, Kanika's gaze flew to her husband's face, but he—as always—remained impassive, as he asked, "What sort of offer, sir?"

"It has come to my attention that you seek a different position."

"And how is that, sir?" The Commander's words were clipped, and it was clear he was not best pleased, that word had leaked out.

"It is my business to know things. And you needn't glower; such a thing was not unexpected, certainly, in light of these events, and in light of your marriage to this redoubtable woman."

In irony, he bowed his head to Kanika, and she—nothing loath—graciously bowed back.

He continued, "The Crown could use a man of your talents. Funding is scarce—scarcer now, thanks to your bride—and the war will resume, soon. We will need someone to supervise the logistics for Wellington's army, and run the operations as close to the bone as we can possibly manage."

There was a small silence, and then her husband turned to meet Kanika's eyes. She could see immediately that he would like to accept this offer very much, and, after all, it made little difference to her—the means, by which he would help his country, in their war. And so, she smiled slightly, and nodded.

The Commander turned back to the grey-eyed man. "I accept. My only condition is that my wife accompany me, wherever I am sent."

The other man glanced at Kanika, and then replied, "Very well. But I will have your oath—on your honor —that you will no longer protect her, if she stirs rebellion against the British."

"You will have my oath," Kanika replied. I am a Kshatriya of Nair, and no one speaks for me, save me."

"Very well; then you will be hearing from me, and sooner rather than later."

He then nodded to Hahn, who'd been a silent witness to the conversation. "You," the grey-eyed man said, as he pulled on his gloves. "You're to come with me."

"Are you speaking to me?" asked Hahn in surprise.

"I am. You will come work for me. If I am any judge of such things, you will enjoy yourself immensely."

"You can't work for him, Hahn," Kanika exclaimed, in astonished outrage. "He nearly had us killed."

But Hahn was unable to suppress a grin. "I bear no grudges, Neeka."

"But—but he is *British*, Hahn," she reminded him, in the event he'd forgot.

"A case of the pot and the kettle," the grey-eyed man chided her. "You married an Englishman. And the Reverend Paisley is an Englishman, yet you had no qualms, working for him."

Kanika stared in surprise. "How—how did you know this?"

"I may have mentioned that it is my job, to know things. In fact, I attempted to recruit the good Reverend, but he declined my offer—something foolish, about the ends not justifying the means." He lifted his brows at Hahn. "I trust you have no such objections."

With a gleam, Hahn asked, "Will I be paid?"

"Handsomely."

"I will do it, then."

"Good. Come along."

And so, Kanika was left standing with the Commander, watching in bemusement, as Hahn followed the grey-eyed man away, the two already engaged in a low-voiced conversation.

Her husband took her hand, and tucked it in his arm. "Perhaps we should sail with Sir Jost, in Hahn's place."

She smiled, slightly. "You are trying to avoid your farewell reception."

"I confess it, readily."

"Yes," she nodded thoughtfully. "Let us sail with the Dutchman."

He leaned to kiss her forehead. "You hold no grudges, either. I don't know as I could be as forgiving, in your place."

But she lifted her head, to meet his eyes. "The Dutchman is not so very terrible—I was wrong, to judge him. And he loves his wife—you can hear it in his voice, when he speaks of her."

"Yes, he does. I believe he met her here, at Fort William."

She raised her brows. "Did he? That is surprising—that he met his wife, in such an ordinary fashion."

Chuckling, he drew her close to his side, as they gazed out the window. "Nowhere near as dramatic, as when I met my wife—fresh from a disaster of her own causing."

She leaned her head against his arm. "I thought you very handsome. It was a pleasant surprise."

"I thought you were trouble, and I was right."

"I was supposed to seduce you," she confessed. "I didn't do a very good job."

"On the contrary; you succeeded beyond all expectations."

But she shook her head, slightly. "No—that is not true; instead, I think we have played to a draw."

He rested his head on hers. "Are you ready, for the next game? I am worried that Europe will seem very strange, to you."

This was true; she'd be a stranger in a strange land, amongst people who were fighting a war that was—for once—not hers. But nevertheless, she didn't hesitate. "I will go wherever you go."

Softly, he prompted, "I will go wherever you go, James."

She smiled. "James."

"This is going to take some doing," he teased.

She sighed. "It is hard to let go of the old ways, even though I know I must." Reminded, she lifted her face to his. "Could we ask the Dutchman to stop at Tellicherry Fort? I would like to introduce you to the Reverend Paisley."

But her husband could be seen to hesitate. "The Reverend may not be best pleased to make my acquaintance."

She smiled, and returned her gaze to the window. "No—you mistake the matter. We will sit in his garden —his cat on his lap—and he will be very pleased to meet you. He has said, many times, that the best stories are stories of redemption."

"Oh? Did I redeem you, or did you redeem me?"

She considered this. "We will leave it for him to decide."

"I will do it, then."

"And I have another request, James."

He leaned to kiss her. "Do you? You are lucky you have an indulgent husband."

"Do you think we can purchase a sailing boat?"

"After the war," he agreed. "And then we will sail wherever you wish."

Nodding, she raised her gaze, to consider the stars. "I would like to sleep on the deck."

There was a small pause. "Right. We can try it, I suppose—I confess I don't have fond memories."

Winding her hands around his arm, she rose on tiptoe, to whisper in his ear, "Then we must make fond memories, James."